PRAISE FOR GLOR

"Sizzling intimacy that will draw you in and continue to keep you enthralled until the final page is turned."
—*The Book Enthusiast*

"Nelle is up there with the best, such as Sylvia Day and E.L. James."
—*Goodreads Review*

"*Gloria's Secret* is a very sexy read that will have you turning the pages trying to fit all the pieces together."
—*Stick Girl Book Reviews*

"This book is emotional, steamy, and wonderfully written."
—*Winding Stairs Book Blog*

"Extremely sexy and extremely provocative, but it also has a plot...a hot, sexy, beautiful and suspenseful read."
—*The Book Hooker*

"Loved it right from the start!...Awesome female lead...HOT male lead...killer secondary characters."
—*The Book Blog*

"I immediately fell for Gloria...I was swept away to her world of haute couture lingerie...Gloria's Secret is above all a romance."
—*Arianne Richmonde,*
Bestselling author of The Pearl Series

BOOKS BY NELLE L'AMOUR

Seduced by the Park Avenue Billionaire

Undying Love

Gloria's Secret

Gloria's Revenge

Dewitched (writing as E.L. Sarnoff)

Unhitched (writing as E.L. Sarnoff)

GLORIA'S SECRET

GLORIA'S SECRET

Nelle L'Amour

NICHOLS CANYON PRESS
Los Angeles, CA USA

Gloria's Secret
By Nelle L'Amour

ISBN-13: 978-1494315191
ISBN-10: 149431519X

Cover and Interior: Streetlight Graphics

Dedicated to all the amazing book bloggers who work selflessly and passionately to bring our books into the hands of readers. I applaud you.

GLORIA'S SECRET

"Rien ne pèse tant qu'un secret."
　　　　　　　　—Jean de La Fontaine

Prologue

Fifteen years earlier...

D ARKNESS SHROUDS US. WE PROWL like two cats, my eyes darting left and right, my ears attuned to even the slightest sound.

I nervously tap my partner in crime's shoulder. Like me, he's clad in black sweats and a hoodie, along with black gloves and athletic shoes. Identical black ski masks cover our faces. We blend into the thick opaque air, only the whites of our eyes visible.

"Kev, I'm scared. Maybe we should back out," I whisper. My heart's thudding in my ears, and I can feel sweat beads clustering on my flesh.

He squeezes my hand. It's cold and clammy beneath my gloves. "Glorious, we've come this far. There's no turning back."

Something scuttles across my shoes. I jump. Kevin beams the flashlight he's holding onto the floor. Phew! It's only a mouse.

The seconds feel like hours. The safe, Kevin assures me, is only steps away. It feels like miles. Kevin swings the flashlight until it lands on the huge vault in front of us. All slick, polished steel, it's bigger than I imagined—a massive, towering fortress.

"Hold this." Kevin hands me the flashlight. I try hard to calm my trembling hands as I watch Kevin rotate the fist-size combination lock.

Right. *Click*. Right again. *Click*. Left. *Click*. Right. *Click*.

"Bingo!"

My thundering heart practically leaps out of my chest when the heavy door springs open. My eyes grow round, filling the apertures of the ski mask. Bundles of one hundred dollar bills are stashed inside, stuffing the safe to the hilt.

Kevin instantly starts shoveling them into his large satchel. I'm paralyzed with shock and fear.

"Glorious, what are you waiting for?"

No matter how much I will them, I can't get my hands to move. The stacks of green bills beckon me, but this feels wrong. So, so wrong. *What am I doing here?*

Kevin continues to recklessly shovel handfuls of the neatly tied up green bundles into his canvas bag.

"C'mon, we've gotta work fast." His voice sounds frantic.

Reluctantly, I crouch down and extend an unsteady hand into the safe. The touch of the raw money burns my fingertips. *I can't do this! I can't!*

An ear-deafening siren sounds. Hot infrared lights flash. The effect is dizzying. An inner panic button goes off inside me as all air leaves my lungs.

"Fuck!" shouts Kevin. "We've gotta get of here."

"Leave the money," I plead.

"No. It's ours. *Yours.*"

No choice. Each grabbing a handle of the heavy, money-laden satchel, we sprint toward the exit.

Heavy footsteps. Not ours. The glaring ray of a flashlight beams into my eyes, blinding me. "What the fuck are you doing here?" The booming, accented voice echoes in the chamber. We're doomed!

"Nobody steals from Boris Borofsky."

"Fuck you," Kevin shouts back.

A powerful arm grips my neck. I open my mouth to scream, but no sound comes out. The other hand rips off my ski mask. My platinum tresses tumble out.

He fists a handful of my hair, yanking my head back. His wretched pink eyes clash with mine, one blue and the other brown.

"You little cunt!" growls the accented voice through clenched teeth. "You're going to pay for this, *seka!*"

"And so are you, bitch," spits Kevin.

Something hard presses into my chest, just above my heart.

Kevin wrenches me free from my assailant but not before a deafening boom explodes in my ear. A scorching white fire shoots through my body. *Oh the pain!*

"You mother fucker." My Kevin.

I feel my body sag as another shot is fired.

"FUUUUUUCK!" A roar like a wounded lion, not mine.

"Oh, Glorious!" cries Kevin as he lifts me in his arms.

The world inside my head fades to black.

Chapter 1

I WAS RUNNING LATE. I WAS never late. "Late" wasn't part of my vocabulary. Damn that breakfast meeting. My guest, the stiff-lipped, balding head of a major Madison Avenue ad agency, showed up forty-five minutes late. There'd been a cab accident on Madison Avenue that had caused a traffic jam. The unexpected had no place in my life. To make matters worse, I had to run back up to my hotel room because I'd carelessly left my cell phone in a different handbag. As the CEO of Gloria's Secret, one of the largest retail emporiums in the world, I couldn't be without my lifeline for the rest of the day.

Clutching my Chanel briefcase in my right hand, I anxiously pressed the elevator "Down" button several times with the other. I was staying in New York City at The Walden, a recently renovated five-star, thirty-story Park Avenue hotel that dated back to the fifties. Unfortunately, my favorite hotel, The Ritz Carlton, was booked up, so I had decided to give this new, highly-rated venue a chance. So far, I hadn't been disappointed. The accommodations were outstanding as was the service.

The elevator, to my relief, arrived quickly. I dashed inside the sleek car, that still retained some of its mid-century charm, and hit the "L" button for the lobby. The polished metal doors slid closed. Just before they met in the middle, a manicured masculine hand flashed between them, preventing them from closing.

In a panic, I fumbled to press the "Open" button, fearing that the doors would slam shut on the hand and crush it. I'd seen this uncanny thing happen once before as a child and had never forgotten the gory scene. Flustered, I lost grip of my stuffed briefcase, and it tumbled onto the floor. In my haste to make it to my next meeting on time, I'd forgotten to zip it. This was just not my day. The contents—dozens of photos of gorgeous supermodels clad in skimpy underwear—scattered around my black Louboutin stilettos. Damn it! I just didn't need this right now. I crouched down to gather up the spillage—no easy task in my tight pencil skirt and six-inch heels. As I began to frantically collect the photos, two loafer-clad feet appeared before my eyes.

"Let me help you." The voice was virile, velvety, and deep.

Before I could blink an eye, I was facing the intruder who had caused me to drop my briefcase. He had bent down to help me gather the loose photos. Our eyes stayed locked onto one another. Mine shooting daggers his way. His deflecting every one of my visual assaults. Just a palm's width apart, I felt his warm breath heat my cheeks and could smell a hint of his deliciously spicy cologne. I recognized it immediately. *Homme,* which means "man" in French. It was part of our newly launched men's line of fragrances. The perfect gift for a woman to give to her man this coming Valentine's Day.

I studied his face and what I could glean of his body. Let's put it this way: I had seen a lot of male models, but this guy was something else. Manly. Built. Mid to late thirties. He was one hundred percent pure gorgeousness with his broad shoulders, intense denim blue eyes, mop of silky chestnut hair, and strong dimpled chin. A fine layer of stubble laced his olive complexion. Along with sockless suede loafers, he was wearing a battered leather bomber jacket over a white cotton tee that showed off his taut chest, and faded designer jeans that revealed a ridge of muscles along his thighs. I assumed his legs were long, but it was hard to tell in his squatting position. What I could tell for sure was that there was a sizeable package between them. My gaze shifted quickly back to the floor.

"Interesting photos," my companion mused, his eyes lingering on a particularly sexy one of a D-cup model fondling her lace-encased breasts. A wry smile twisted on his lips. "Hmm. I think I fucked her once." He picked up another. "She looks familiar too."

"Give me those!" I snatched the photos from him and slipped them into my briefcase.

"Are you a photographer?" he asked, not the least bit intimidated by me.

"Hardly."

"So, you're some kind of pervert who collects photos of beautiful semi-naked women with big tits."

"And you're some kind of pervert who sleeps with them." I shot him my dirtiest look and continued collecting the scattered photos. We both reached for the last one, and my hand brushed up against his. God, his hand was beautiful! Large, long-fingered, and so, so soft. Even the violet veins that splayed across them were works of art.

Caught in the moment, I suddenly realized we weren't moving. The elevator doors were still open. In my flustered state, I'd forgotten to hit the "Close" button.

"Would you mind hitting the 'Close' button?" My voice was edgy.

"Good idea. Places to go; people to meet." He rose to his feet. My eyes roamed up his long, athletic legs. He was easily six foot three. A magnificent pillar of leanness and muscle.

With his long forefinger, he pushed the button, and the doors glided together. The elevator descended, but before I could stand up, it came to a jolting halt. I felt the onset of a mini panic attack. My heart raced and sweat pooled behind my knees. I hated being out of control.

"Are you okay?" asked the mysterious stranger, crouching down again.

I gulped. Unable to find my voice, I nodded like one of those bobble head dolls. The truth: I was losing it, and I wasn't sure if it was the effect his gorgeousness was having on me or that of the erratic elevator.

He brushed my chin with the tip of my long platinum braid. "Don't worry. This happens all the time with this elevator."

Without warning, the elevator jerked and began to free fall. I gasped.

"Hey, we're moving again. This is an express elevator, so we'll be down in no time."

My heart dropped to my stomach even faster. This man was having a very uncomfortable effect on me. I felt my cheeks heat and my heart tick like a metronome.

In no time, the elevator reached our destination, and the doors opened wide. My companion lifted me to my feet. His firm grip around my shoulders made me tingle. We stood face-to-face. My five foot seven inch frame in six-inch heels confirmed his estimated height. Standing erect, his body was even more imposing than I'd imagined. His shoulders were square, his hips narrow, and his legs long and solid.

"Ladies, first," he said with a sexy wink.

With my briefcase in hand, I shot out of the elevator and walked briskly through the bustling mid-century themed lobby to the entrance of the hotel. The clickety-clack of my heels across the marble floor echoed in my ears. Mr. Infuriating strode next to me, keeping up with my pace with ease.

Outside the tall, glass and steel building, we stood side by side. The early morning rush of New York pedestrians and cabs passed us by. The weather was picture-postcard perfect and surprisingly mild for a mid-February day. I was glad that I didn't wear a coat.

"Can I give you a ride?" he asked. "My driver will be here any minute."

"I have my own driver," I replied without looking his way.

"Impressive." I didn't miss the playful sarcasm in his voice.

His driver, in a sleek black Ranger Rover, pulled up first. A hotel valet raced to open the back door for my companion.

"See ya." He winked at me again.

Bastard!

With a roguish smirk, he slid into the Rover. His eyes lingered on mine before the passenger door closed. My deadpan face didn't move a muscle as the car pulled away.

Two minutes later, my black town car pulled up. My driver stepped out and escorted me into the back seat.

"Good morning, Miss Long."

"Good morning, Nigel," I said brightly as I sidled gracefully into the car. Trusty Nigel was always my driver when I came to New York for business. I could always count on the jovial, silver-haired Brit to get me anywhere. And there on time.

"Where to this morning?"

I gave him the address of ZAP! It was located in the heart of Soho.

I leaned back into the comfy leather seat and let out a sigh. This was the tenth—and last advertising agency—I was visiting. Since the beginning of the week, I had met with all of the top Madison Avenue ad agencies. It had been a draining, whirlwind tour.

Truthfully, none of them had impressed me. As CEO of Gloria's Secret, the largest lingerie retail chain in the world, I was looking for a creative team to help me bring my empire to a new level of sensuality and sales. With the insane popularity of books like

Fifty Shades of Grey, I was convinced women were looking for a new way to express themselves. A way that communicated: *Take me—I'm yours.* If we were going to stay ahead of the competition, then I had to be the first to tap into this hot, new erotic trend. We were already developing a line of provocative products.

The car cruised down Fifth Avenue, Nigel expertly weaving in and out of the maddening midtown traffic. In the back seat, I mused about my upcoming meeting.

Unlike the other ad agencies I'd visited, ZAP! was a relatively new kid on the block. What was called a "boutique agency."

Several things I'd read online about it had impressed me. First, they had created a campaign for a new Japanese minivan that made the word "minivan" sexy. The campaign's tagline: *And the mommy goes 'mmmmmmmm.'* Anyone who could turn an oppressive minivan into a sexy beast scored points with me.

Secondly, the founder and CCO (Chief Creative Officer) of the agency was a woman. Jaime Zander. Our new advertising campaign needed the touch of a woman. Someone who had insight into women's sexual desires and fantasies. Someone who had read *Fifty Shades of Grey* and understood its phenomenal success. I, too, was drawn to the sexy, enigmatic Christian Grey and believed that our new BDSM-inspired undergarments would give a woman a better chance at landing her own Mr. Grey. Or, at least, let her fantasize she could.

Lastly, I was drawn to the ZAP! website. It was

innovative and creative rather than corporate and boastful. I especially liked the key personnel profile photos—all adorable baby pictures, including CCO Jaime, with her head full of chestnut curls, sweet dimpled chin, and checkered overalls.

Nigel dropped me off in front of a brick townhouse on Prince Street. I double-checked the address on my iPhone, thinking that ZAP! might be housed in slightly more corporate headquarters. But sure enough, this was where the agency was located. My courteous driver opened the passenger door for me. Hopping out, I told him I would call him after the meeting was over.

Once inside the building, I stepped into the reception area. Unlike the stark, leather and chrome waiting areas of the Madison Avenue *Madmen* agencies I'd met with, this one was warm and funky, filled with eccentric mid-century furnishings and a shag carpet that reminded me a little of the hotel I was staying at. The blazing orange letters—ZAP!— were hung like giant puzzle pieces on the bright yellow wall behind the receptionist's jet-age console. She was an artsy-looking girl in her early twenties who sported a graphic Jim Morrison tee and several tattoos on her bare arms. She was a far cry from the impeccably groomed young women who manned the front desk at those other ad agencies I'd visited.

"I have a ten o'clock meeting with Jaime Zander," I told her.

She glanced at her computer screen and asked me if I was Gloria Long.

"Yes."

"Cool."

She dialed an extension, announcing my arrival to whoever was on the receiving end. I assumed it was Jaime's assistant. "Someone will be right out to bring you back to Jaime's office. Make yourself comfy."

Before I could take a seat on the elliptical couch, a twenty-something man with inky blue hair and an earring sashayed into the reception area to fetch me. He was very attractive, very stylish, and very gay. He smiled brightly at me, revealing a set of perfect white teeth. "I'm Ray, Jaime's assistant. Jaime is so looking forward to meeting you. Follow me."

Though younger, he reminded me a lot of my best friend and head of Public Relations, Kevin Riley, who was uptown at the Lexington Avenue Armory preparing for the highly anticipated pre-Valentine's Day Gloria's Secret Fashion Show. My assistant, Vivien Holden, was there too. Right after this meeting, I would be rushing uptown to join them. As always on one of these business trips to New York, we had a hell of a lot going on. In fact, too much. The sooner I got out of New York, the better. Boris Borofsky was lurking out there somewhere. Inwardly, I shuddered.

With my briefcase in hand, I followed hip-swaying Ray through a gutted space to the end office. I liked the way everyone sat in the open and was immersed in their work. My eyes took in the posters for various ad campaigns that lined the walls. Most of them were familiar and indeed quite memorable.

"Jaime had to run down the hall to check out a spot we just produced for one of our clients and will be right back. Can I get you anything to drink?"

"I'm fine, thank you," I said, surveying my surroundings and deciding where to sit. I chose a Scandinavian armchair over the couch. Sitting tall and cross-legged in a chair was always more empowering than sitting laid back in a couch. I liked to be in control of a meeting, especially when it was with someone I didn't know.

My eyes toured the expansive office. Like the reception area, it was warm and funky, filled with eccentric, colorful, artsy furnishings. Intriguing abstract portraits and landscapes dotted the walls, all signed PAZ; one of the portraits was of a blue-eyed baby girl that looked a lot like the photo I'd seen online. My favorite piece of furniture was Jaime's desk which was shaped like a large kidney bean. For a busy CCO, she had few things on it. Just a stack of neatly arranged bright-colored files, a state-of-the-art Apple computer, and a single framed photo. Behind the desk was a credenza that displayed the many awards the small advertising agency had garnered. From what I'd gleaned of Jaime's taste so far, she must be quite a creative and interesting woman. I was looking forward to meeting her and getting down to business.

With a few minutes to spare, I used the time to my advantage. Pulling out my iPhone from my handbag, I checked my e-mails. There were easily a hundred new ones from people who reported to me around the world. From store managers to subcontractors. Why did everyone have to bother me with their silly problems? But that was my job. To run the company. There were only two that I urgently needed to read. The first, from Kevin, who was likely updating me about the status of this afternoon's annual Gloria's Secret Fashion Show. I opened it and sucked in a deep breath. So far everything was on schedule and moving forward. The other one was good news too. It was from one of my product managers informing me that the first prototype of the sex toys we were developing had been shipped to our Los Angeles headquarters. A smile spread across my face. We were about to expand our business, which now included intimate apparel, active wear, and beauty products, with a collection of BDSM-inspired lingerie and a complementary line of fun, innovative sex toys. Our consumer research with focus groups had strongly indicated that this could be a breakout piece of business for us—women believed that vibrators, dildoes, and bondage accessories, like lace masks and silk handcuffs, were a natural extension of our already sexy product line. And that Gloria's Secret was a store where they would feel comfortable purchasing these provocative items. We had indeed evolved into a major lifestyle brand. As I was about to hit reply, an urgent e-mail came in from Kevin.

G~

The run-through was HOT! Except the lead model tripped on her heels and sprained her ankle. Looking for a replacement. Challenging as all models are working Fashion Week. Will keep you posted.

~K

I replied to his e-mail with a smiley face emoticon. Among the many things I loved about Kevin was that he was a problem solver. He had once saved my life. If it weren't for him, I wouldn't be who I am; there would be no Gloria's Secret. I was confident he would find a replacement, and the show would go on. I began to reply to the remaining e-mails.

The sound of sprightly footsteps diverted my attention. My head swiveled to the doorway. My mouth dropped to the floor, and my iPhone slipped out of my hand. Oh. My. God. It was him! That pompous asshole who had caused me to drop my briefcase in the elevator and then played head games with me. What the hell was he doing here? Maybe he worked for Ms. Zander?

He took long confident steps in my direction. I hesitantly stood up. He took my hand in his and shook it. His grip was firm, the touch warm and smooth. My body stiffened and my heartbeat quickened.

"Gloria, a pleasure to meet you officially."

I wasn't sure if I had yet closed my mouth, but I was speechless. I finally found my voice. "And you're..."

"Jaime Zander."

Fuck! Holy, holy, fuck!

I collapsed back into my chair. He shot me a devilish smile. Damn him. He knew I was caught off guard. Big time.

Wordlessly, I gazed up at his face. The baby photo that I'd seen online flashed into my head. It was him all right. Though maybe thirty-five years older, he had the same baby blue eyes with that thick fan of lashes, silky chestnut hair, and that distinct dimpled chin. He had been one of those babies that old ladies would look at and say, "Oh, he's pretty enough to be a girl."

Mortification struck me like a lightning bolt. I was not easily rattled, but Mr. Zander had succeeded. I suddenly didn't want to do the meeting or give him my business.

Paralyzed, my eyes stayed locked on him as he lowered himself into the chair catty-cornered to mine. We were in such close proximity that I could inhale the intoxicating scent of him and feel his warm breath on my cheeks.

"Are you sure I can't get you something? A coffee? Water? Tea perhaps?"

A fan?

"No, thank you," I said, nervously tugging on the thick, flaxen braid that wrapped around my shoulder and cascaded over my boobs. The sooner we got down to business the better. His presence was making me bristle. *Get a grip, Gloria. You're one of Forbes's One Hundred Most Powerful Women in the World!*

Composing myself, I began by telling him that I was seeking an outside agency to bring my company, Gloria's Secret, to a new level of sales and sensuality.

He folded one long, muscled leg over the other and relaxed back in his chair with his sculpted forearms casually crossed over his crotch—I mean, lap. "Gloria's Secret. The #1 lingerie retailer in the world. 2,045 stores worldwide. Estimated annual sales revenue: 6.2 billion dollars."

He had indeed done his homework. But there was no way in hell that I was going to let him know that I was impressed. My expression remained impassive while I responded.

"Yes. We've enjoyed phenomenal success. But we can't stop here. Imitators are springing up. We've got to stay on the cutting edge, ahead of the competition." I paused. Okay, now the test. "Did you read *Fifty Shades of Grey*?"

He grinned. "Of course."

Ha! I didn't believe him. He was bullshitting me. I could tell by the wry look on his face.

"Okay, then what's the full name of Christian Grey's adoptive mother?"

"Are you testing me, Gloria?"

"It's Ms. Long, and yes, I am...Well?"

Without wasting a second, he said, "Grace Trevelyn Grey. And she's a pediatrician."

Damn it! Score one for him. Except for one feminist copywriter who pooh-poohed the book for demeaning women, none of the Madison Avenue suits had read it. I had to hand it to him. But exam time wasn't over yet. "Mr. Zander—"

"Please call me Jaime."

"All right, *Jai-me*, tell me, what, in your opinion, has made the book so popular with women?"

He leaned into me, looking straight into my eyes. His gaze was mesmerizing. As much as I wanted to divert my eyes, they stayed on him.

"Truthfully, while the sex is hot, I believe women fall for the romance."

"What do you mean?" I was all ears.

"Well, *Ms. Long*, wouldn't you like me to scoop you up in my arms...tell you that 'I want you, body and soul, forever' and make insane love to you on the couch?"

Inwardly, I gasped. He had actually quoted Christian Grey. My eyes took in his mountainous biceps, jumped to the couch, and then back to his crotch. My temperature had just risen ten degrees. Confession: I had the burning urge to shrug off more than just my suit jacket.

He leaned in closer and growled into my ear. "Or would you prefer me to throw you over my desk... or perhaps carry you away and devour you on the conference room table down the hall?"

I squeezed my inner thighs together and could not stop my crossed leg from swinging like a pendulum—a behavior that was so not in my repertoire. I jerked away from him and found my voice. "You seem to know women rather well."

He sat back in the chair. "Yes, I do." His tone was confident, almost cocky.

"In my experience, the only men who understand women are gay. Are you, by chance, gay, Jaime?"

He let out a deep, sexy chortle. "Hardly. I could have several hundred stunning women give you a stellar recommendation."

"Oh, so you have them review you like you're a book on Amazon?" My deadpan sarcasm camouflaged my shock at the number of women he'd likely fucked.

He laughed again. "You're quite witty, Ms. Long. I like that in a woman."

Again, I was speechless. Damn him!

He moved in again uncomfortably close to me and snagged my braid, coiling it around his lithe, long-fingered hand. "So, what will it take to win your account?"

The hair play was angsting me out. And so was

his proximity. I promptly removed his hand from my tresses and composed myself once more. "I've asked every agency I've met with to come up with a pitch by Friday. Do you think your agency could do that?"

"Not a problem. I'll put my best person on the job right away."

"And who might that be?" I asked, my voice dripping with a mix of curiosity and sarcasm.

He grinned wickedly. "Yours truly." With that, he rose and escorted me to the door. Before I could step over the threshold, he barricaded it with his body and outstretched arms. His biceps flexed as he pressed his hands against the framework. We were face-to-face again, only a breath away.

His eyes bore a hole in mine. "I meant to tell you, Ms. Long, I find your eyes fascinating."

Most people did. My right eye was blue; my left one brown. I had a rare genetic condition known as heterochromia. In press releases and on the Internet, both eyes appeared to be brown thanks to Photoshop. But because I suffered from dry eye syndrome, I was unable to use contacts to conceal my idiosyncrasy the rest of the time.

Jaime continued to study my mismatched eyes. "They're contradictions just like the rest of you."

That I hadn't heard before. "What do you mean?"

"Your mind says one thing, your body says another."

His words spurred a rush of tingles to my core and sent my heart into a gallop. Damn him! He was unhinging me again. "Mr. Zander, can I please leave?" I spluttered.

With a smirk, he pivoted so that he was leaning

against the doorway. He gave my braid a little tug as I hurried past him. "Ms. Long, I look forward to the *pleasure* of seeing you again."

"The same." *Bastard!*

As I stomped down the hallway, I could feel his fiery eyes on my backside. His voice traveled down the corridor. "Oh, by the way, I find your black lace push-up bra and matching thong very sexy. And that garter..."

Cringing, I just kept moving. How the hell did he know what I was wearing under my Chanel suit?

Chapter 2

INSANITY. UTTER INSANITY. THAT WAS the only way to describe the electrifying pre-show atmosphere at the Lexington Avenue Armory. Production personnel were running around like banshees getting it together. They were talking into headsets and cell phones and frantically jotting down notes on clipboards and in notebooks. The look of stress and panic was etched on everyone's faces. The adrenaline was flying. The much-anticipated Gloria's Secret Fashion Show was scheduled to start in an hour, but it seemed like we'd never get there.

It was always like this even though this was our tenth show. This one, however, was more ambitious because it was celebrating our first decade of putting them on. For the first time, the show was being broadcast on a major television network in addition to being shown live on our website. Every fashion journalist and blogger in the world was going to be here including reporters from *Entertainment Tonight...Vogue...*Joan and Melissa Rivers...even that teenage wunderkind blogger, Tavi Gevinson... just to name a few. And the celebrity list was endless.

"Glorious! Thank God, you're here!" a familiar breathless voice called out. It was my trusted head of PR and Special Events, Kevin Riley. Kevin and

I had been best friends forever. Since childhood. We knew everything about each other and shared a dark secret that bonded us eternally. We had been through a lot, and never for a minute did I forget that I owed so much of my success to him. In fact, my life. I loved him like a brother. We even had nicknames for one and other. I called him Kev, and he called me Glorious. We'd built Gloria's Secret from the ground up together.

"What's going on?" I asked as he jogged up to me. While Kev could be an outrageous dresser (I'm talking kilts and jumpsuits), today he was dressed for functionality in perfectly shredded black jeans, a tight V-neck tee, and high-top Keds. With his spiky, dark-haired good looks, svelte toned body, and charismatic smile, he could easily make women melt, but that was not his preference. The diamond ear stud that he proudly wore said it all. It had been a birthday gift from me.

With a flutter of his deep-set hazel eyes, he sighed, "The usual. The models are having meltdowns over who's wearing what...Kim Kardashian's people just called saying she's miffed that she's not in the front row...and Rihanna's limo is stuck in traffic."

I rolled my eyes. There was no need to freak. All these hiccups were routine for this show. Business as usual. I trusted Kevin implicitly with my heart and soul. He'd make sure things worked out. They always did.

His cell phone rang. He put it to his ear and said, "Great." Smiling, he ended the call. "Rihanna's here! Gotta go." He gave me a peck on my cheek. "Glorious, this show is going to rock!"

God, I loved Kev! He brought good luck and sunshine even in the darkest times. As he scurried off, my eyes drank in everything. This show *was* going to rock! The set designer that Kevin had hired had created an outrageous fantasy of a sexed-up heaven. Dry smoke surfaced from the stage floor and rose up to the high ceiling where virtual clouds were projected. The plan was for dozens of gorgeous Gloria's Secret models, clad in outrageous angel wings and the barest of bare undergarments, to float down from the ceiling via invisible ropes onto the runway. Some would even be entwined with sexy male angels in hot embraces. We were selling sex—fantasies and wet dreams. I so loved it! If the televised show went off without a hitch and got high ratings, tomorrow—Valentine's Day—would be our stores' busiest day of the year and lead to record first quarter earnings.

While I took in everything and contemplated my mandatory end-walk down the runway, another familiar, this time shrill feminine voice, sounded in my ear.

"If you don't do it my way, I'm going to have you fired." It was Vivien Holden, my assistant, arguing with a tired, overworked production assistant. I didn't need to spin around because she was already in my face.

She was clad in a hot pink Gloria's Secret mini skirt that barely covered her ass, a crisp white blouse opened far enough to reveal her eye-worthy cleavage, and six-inch black patent stilettos that made her compact busty body rise to almost five foot six. I had to admit Vivien was stunning; she was younger than me by four years. I was thirty-three, she, twenty-nine. Her blessings, albeit manufactured, included a mane of long thick ebony hair (weaves), full, sensuous lips (filler), piercing green eyes (contacts), and a perfect upturned nose that I suspected was the result of plastic surgery along with her D-cup boobs. She could afford to have her features altered. She was rich. Mega rich. "Daddy"— billionaire corporate raider, Victor Holden—was Gloria's Secret's largest shareholder and Chairman of the Board. I could never keep track of how many shares he controlled. All I needed to remember was that he could make or break everything I'd built. And make or break me.

Despite being my assistant, Vivien was never pleased to see me. She narrowed her catty eyes and gave me the once-over. "How did it go today with ZAP!?"

Before I could respond, she huffed, "You know, Gloria, I should have been there. Daddy says advertising is soon going to be under my domain."

Her words irked me. Everything was under *my* domain. I was the CEO and founder of Gloria's Secret. Vivien thought she was entitled because Daddy backed the company. Though she was talented, she wanted to get to the top quickly. It was no secret that she coveted my job. Inhaling deeply, I controlled myself. I couldn't afford to offend her because of her father. It was sort of a Catch-22 situation that I had to accept.

"No, Vivien, you belonged here. The Gloria's Secret Fashion Show can make or break our year-end earnings. Plus, there's so much you can learn from being on the set."

She scoffed at me. "The only thing I've learned is that I'm surrounded by a bunch of incompetent morons."

God, I wanted to slap her. Or rip off her phony lips. And that was not all.

With a flick of her head, she flung back her mane of hair, one of her annoying habits. "So what was Jaime Zander like? I haven't seen him for years."

My brows lifted. Vivien knew Jaime? Why didn't she tell me? She could have spared me a lot of embarrassment.

"He was very professional," I answered, masking my displeasure. She had no need to know the details of the meeting. The thought of Jaime Zander made my breathing hitch. "I'm looking forward to his pitch, which I want you and Kevin to attend."

Her cat green eyes lit up. "And I'm looking forward to seeing him again."

She sauntered off before I could I ask her what she meant by that.

"In five, four, three, two, one...Showtime!" Hot techno music blasted; my heart hammered. Watching from backstage, I gaped as our gorgeous long-legged supermodel angels, their D-cup bodies clad in the skimpiest lace bras and thongs, descended from the ceiling through a cloud of dry ice onto the runway and began to strut down it, one after another, in their six-inch stilettos. Their outrageous colorful feathered wings, attached to their backs, fluttered like butterflies as they vamped to the beat of the pulsing music. Loud gasps, whistles, and applause emanated from the celebrity-packed audience and press. I let out a deep breath. Yes! They loved it! My beloved Kevin had pulled it off again. It truly was an unforgettable spectacle. Almost surreal, otherworldly. I was totally in the moment but wouldn't be relaxed until it was over. Every muscle in my body clenched.

Twenty minutes into the show, Kevin joined me backstage. While I was still an exposed nerve waiting for the worst to happen, he was like a child in a candy store. His long-lashed hazel eyes lit up like lanterns. "It's faaabulous!" he crooned, squeezing my hand. In my anxious state, his hand was a welcome comfort.

"Have you seen Vivien?" I asked.

"Not for ages."

I wondered where she was. She was supposed to be with me, updating me on the live webcast. Once things settled down and we were back in Los Angeles, I was going to have a come to Jesus meeting with her, regardless of who her father was. That girl needed to learn what it meant to be a team player.

Without a hitch, the show continued to blow the audience away. Oohs, aahs, whistles, and cheers filled the air. Forty minutes in, Rihanna descended from "the heavens" in a cloud of pink smoke. The crowd went wild. She looked amazing, her dazzling body clad in a diamond-studded black leather bra and thong that we had custom-made for her. The cost to make the ensemble was one million dollars, but it was being auctioned off later tonight for charity at the after-party that Vivien's father, Victor Holden, was hosting at Touch. My hunch was that some billionaire pervert was going to buy the matching set and put them to his nose every night at bedtime. I chortled silently.

With raw sexuality, Rihanna belted out her new song, "Open Your Mind." *Mind over body; body over mind. Open your legs wide. Baby, let him know you're mine.* Closing my eyes, I found myself thrusting my hips, getting lost in the words and beat of the stunning superstar's sensuous song. Without warning, the image of a stunning man flooded my head. Jaime Zander! We were face-to-face. Heart to heart. Hip to hip!

My heart was vibrating. And then I realized it was actually my cell phone that I'd stuck inside my shirt pocket. I'd put it on mute, having informed all employees to text me during the show only if it was an emergency. I silently cursed. This must be an emergency. My eyes flew open. I immediately checked my messages.

Ms. Long~
What does this song do for you?
x*J*

The air escaped my lungs. *Holy Shit! He's here?*

With grinding dance moves to match, Rihanna continued to exude sex with her sultry words. My core was pulsing, my heart racing. What was wrong with me? Jaime Zander! This man, who I hardly knew, had no right to invade my head. And stalk me, no less!

"Gloria, it's almost over!" said Kevin, snapping me back to reality.

My mind was elsewhere as Rihanna took a bow, and the show moved into the grand finale. In a file, all the sexy, winged models paraded down the runway, glowing with big smiles on their faces. The audience leaped up from their seats, applauding and cheering as the last model did her turn.

"Glorious, go! It's your turn to take a bow." A remixed version of the late great Laura Branigan's popular 80's song "Gloria" was always my signal... *calling Gloria.* Taking my phone out of my trembling hand, Kevin had to virtually to push me onto the runway. I was so distracted with thoughts of Jaime Zander that I'd forgotten about this mandatory ritual.

Wearing Gloria's Secret black leggings and an oversized button-down white blouse that I'd changed into before the show, I staggered down the runway, my legs like jelly. Thank goodness, I was wearing our popular ballet flats. The models and standing audience applauded and cheered loudly. I inhaled deeply. Once again, I was in the moment, in control. Without a doubt, this show had been our best ever; we had outdone ourselves. Taking my bow, I was both humbled and elated. Fireworks went off, and a flurry of confetti cascaded from the heavens, temporarily blinding me. When the confetti and smoke settled, my eyes grew wide. Sitting in the front row was Vivien. And right next to her, was Jaime Zander, wearing a wicked smile. My gaze met his with a gape, and suddenly I felt as naked as the scantily clad models embracing me.

∞

After the models got back into their own clothes and congratulated me backstage, I searched desperately for Vivien. I was fuming. I needed answers. What the hell was Jaime Zander doing at the fashion show and who had invited him? I had asked Kevin, but he had no clue and was as surprised as I was.

Vivien was nowhere to be found backstage, and she wasn't picking up her cell. I was getting madder by the second, but my bladder was begging a trip to the restroom. I hadn't peed for hours.

I ran to the nearest ladies' room and flew inside. There she was. I should have guessed—in front of a mirror. Leaning into the glass, she pursed her inflated lips as she applied a fresh coat of pink lip-gloss. My reflection met hers.

"Oh, hi, Gloria," she said after smacking her lips. "The show looked great online. We've had two million hits. I bet it's going to get fabulous ratings."

Great. But that was not on my mind at the moment. "What was Jaime Zander doing in the front row?" I asked, followed by a silent question. *And why the hell were you sitting next to him?*

She slipped her tube of lip-gloss back into her quilted Chanel purse and did that obnoxious hair fling. "Oh, I hope you don't mind. I sent him an invitation. I thought it would be good for business. Give him a little edge in terms of winning the Gloria's Secret account."

Inside, I was seething. How dare she go behind my back and invite him without telling me? My eyes narrowed with fury. "You should have told me, Vivien."

She shrugged her shoulders. "Ooh, I'm sorry. I

totally forgot. I was so busy." Her saccharine voice was oozing with phoniness. *Liar!*

I clenched my hands and zipped my mouth. It wasn't worth challenging her because in my heart I knew I'd get nowhere with her; she would just twist and turn things around. I loosened my fingers and splattered some cold water on my face as she shimmied toward the door.

"By the way, Jaime's as gorgeous as ever."

I swiveled around but she was already gone. Damn it! I'd forgotten to ask her how she knew Jaime Zander. I'd also forgotten to pee. Tonight at the after-party, I was going to find out.

Chapter 3

THE GLORIA'S SECRET FASHION SHOW after-party was one of the most coveted invitations in the city. While many would give the shirts off their backs to be invited to the glamorous *New York Post Page Six*-worthy event, I usually found it boring. Lots of A-list beautiful people, wannabes, booze, drugs, and loud music. After the stress of this afternoon's show, I was exhausted. What I really wanted to do was order in room service and curl up in my luxurious bed with a good book on my eReader. But I had no choice. As founder and CEO of Gloria's Secret, I was expected to attend and party like there was no tomorrow.

I considered myself pretty low maintenance and prided myself on how fast I could transform from a high-powered executive to a glamorous night owl. Tonight, however, I was taking my time. I needed to unwind. I poured myself a glass of wine from the mini-bar and then drew myself a hot bath, pouring a capful of fragrant lavender bath salt from our Bed and Bath Collection into the rapidly rising water. Stripped naked, I dimmed the bathroom lights and lit a fragrant Gloria's Secret candle, something I always traveled with on business trips.

Pinning up my braid with a few loose bobby pins

I found on the sink counter, I stepped into the deep tub and sunk into the steamy water. On contact, I let out a loud sigh and felt my tension melt away. I leaned my head against the marble and stretched my legs out long. Reaching for the large sponge, I circled my firm, heavy breasts, brushing over the quarter-sized scar I wore above my heart. I closed my eyes to block out the memory—the secret—that scar harbored. It never worked. I always relived it. I always shuddered. As I swept my hand over my sensitive pink nipples, my mind, unannounced, switched channels from the memory of that horrible night to another unsettling reality show—Jaime Zander!

He was back in my head. I had to admit he was gorgeous. And sexy as sin. The way he looked at me with those intense denim blues was unnerving enough. But when he shot me that cocky smile, I became completely undone. And he knew he affected me. Damn him!

It had to stop. Control was something that I clung to and needed to survive. The thought of losing control petrified me. I had spent hours in therapy dealing with my control issue and the roots of it. Dr. Pepperdine, my shrink, believed it stemmed from my mother...that I feared to become her, a pathetic addict who craved sex as much as she did crack, relying on men to feed her sick habits. In part, she was right. But what she didn't know was that my need for control was attached far more to the scar. The secret. Boris Borofsky was out there somewhere and could take everything that was precious to me away from me. Including my life.

Enough. It was time to step out of the tub and focus on getting ready for the party. With the towel draped around me, I stood before the mirror and did my makeup. My routine was simple, even for a glam night out—mascara, eyeliner, a little blush, and some Gloria's Secret lip-gloss. Refreshed and polished, I padded back to my bed where I'd carefully laid out what I was going to wear. Shedding the towel, I began with my lingerie—an underwire, front-closing black lace bra, matching bikinis, and complementary garter belt—all part of our bestselling "Sexy Nights" collection. I then lowered myself to the bed and languidly inched the sheer lace-trimmed silk stockings up my long, smooth waxed legs. Real silk stockings from Paris were my one non-Gloria's Secret indulgence—a habit I'd inherited from my mentor, Madame Paulette, who I was visiting tomorrow.

I slipped into my dress. Okay, confession. It, too, was not from the Gloria's Secret catalogue. It was a splurgy little black number by Alexander Wang—a designer whose line I admired and wanted to work with down the road. I was thinking of asking him to design a reasonably priced line of dresses for Gloria's Secret the way Target and H&M were approaching top designers. His cutting-edge sexiness was a good fit. There was definitely money to be made.

After pulling up the side zipper of the dress, I stepped into my black satin, red-soled Louboutins, another designer I wanted to approach for a collaboration. Lastly, I grabbed my black pashmina shawl and clutch. Both finds were from Loehmann's Back Room—one of impeccably dressed Madame

Paulette's passed-on secrets. I quickly re-braided my long blond hair and glanced at myself in the floor length mirror opposite the closet. I was pleased. I looked polished and confident. Ready to work the Gloria's Secret after-party.

As I was about to scoot out of my suite, my cell phone rang. I expected it to be from Kevin, who was already likely manning the after-party. Not. Instead, it was from my driver Nigel.

"Miss Long," he said hesitantly, "my daughter's water has prematurely broken."

It took me no time to put two and two together. His beloved only daughter, who was married to a Brooklyn-based writer, was giving birth. I knew what he was going to ask me before he could utter another word.

"Nigel, you must be with her. Get to the hospital right now. I'll just take a cab."

"Are you sure, Miss Long?"

I smiled. We'd been together for a long time. Although he knew nothing about my past, he genuinely cared about me and protected me. I loved him like a godfather.

"Of course. Call me the minute the baby is born."

"Thank you, Miss Long."

"No, thank you, Nigel. Congratulations!"

I sighed as I hung up the phone. At thirty-three years old with no long-term relationship in sight, a baby and a family were likely not going to be mine for the having.

I'd forgotten how hard it was to get a cab during

rush hour in New York City. Make that impossible. It made me appreciate Nigel even more.

Forget who I was. I was lined up behind at least twenty other guests at the hotel's entrance where a valet was desperately trying to hail cabs with the help of an ear-piercing whistle. Occupied cabs kept whooshing by. Shit! At this rate, I'd probably be in line for at least a half hour. I needed to be at the Gloria's Secret party. Now!

"Can I give you a ride?"

The familiar male voice, deep and sexy, purred in my ear as I tightened my fingers around my clutch. I spun around and gawked. It was him! Jaime Zander! What was he doing at the hotel...again? Was he really stalking me? Or was it just a coincidence?

My eyes drank him in. He was wearing another sexy black biker jacket, black tight-ass jeans, a V-neck white tee, and alligator loafers with no socks. Damn! I loved the way he was dressed. My skin prickled and my pulse quickened. *Take a deep breath, Gloria. Breathe!*

"Is that a yes or no, Ms. Long?" He shot me a crooked smile that was daring me to take him up on his offer.

I silently debated if I should. The long cab line hadn't budged an inch. I had little choice. "Fine." I stabbed the word at him like a dart just as his shiny black Range Rover pulled up to the curb. He shuffled me toward the car as his driver opened the back passenger door. I tingled at his warm touch.

"After you." Jaime followed behind me as I gracefully slid into the plush SUV. I sat as far away from him as I could, but he sidled up right next to me. I could feel his warm breath on my neck and smell his heavenly cologne—again our spicy made-for-him fragrance. I suddenly felt lightheaded. Maybe it was the way it mixed with the scent of his skin and the leather of his jacket.

"What were you doing at the fashion show?" I spluttered.

"Research."

"How did you get invited?"

"I have connections."

Vivien?

His denim blue eyes gave me a long once-over. "You look hot."

All at once, I felt hot—make that near the melting point. I crossed one leg over the other, trying to calm the sudden pulsing sensation between them.

"You got a big date tonight?" He brushed the tip of my braid under my chin, coaxing a response.

I squirmed. "I'm going to a Gloria's Secret party at Touch."

That cocky grin curled on his lips. "Then we'll arrive together."

I flinched. "What do you mean?"

"I'm on the A-List."

I mentally grimaced. I bet Vivien had invited him. The little vixen wants to get into his pants. I was going to have to watch her like a hawk tonight. I took a deep calming breath and shot my companion a challenging look.

"Shouldn't you be home or at your office working on the Gloria's Secret pitch? You know, I expect to see it on Friday with my team. That's less than forty-eight hours away."

He let out a deep, sexy laugh. "Oh, I've nailed that already."

"Really?" My voice registered genuine surprise.

"Yeah, you inspire me."

"What else do I do to you?"

"You make me hard."

His words made me jolt. I glanced down at his crotch and my eyes widened. Holy shit! He wasn't kidding. There was a substantial bulge between his legs that was straining against his jeans.

I was still in shock when he grabbed my right hand and placed it on the bump. A hot, rock-hard mound met my palm. Before I could move a finger, he cupped his warm hand over mine, pressing it against his arousal. My pulse was in overdrive, and I was bristling all over.

"Gloria, look at me."

Hesitantly, I turned his way. I met his penetrating gaze.

"I'm not a bullshitter. I want your account. What do I have to do to win it?"

"First, let go of my hand." I spit out the words.

He slowly lifted his hand. My fingers flew off his cock.

He shot me a saucy smile. "What else?"

"Come up with something I love."

"I've got something you'll love, and it's right here in this car."

For a New York minute, I froze, positive he was going to zip down his fly. I didn't know whether to sigh in relief or cry out in frustration when he swung open the door of a built-in cabinet and pulled out a bottle of champagne in an ice bucket along with two flutes. After uncorking the bubbly, he poured us each a glass and proposed a toast.

"To our relationship." He clinked his glass against mine. Normally, I drank very little, but I was in mighty need of a drink. This man was getting under my skin. And I more than liked it.

Chapter 4

THERE WAS ALREADY A MAJOR scene outside when we pulled up to Touch on West Fifty-Second Street. Wannabes were clamoring to get past the bouncers and the red velvet rope, and paparazzi were stepping over each other to get shots of the arriving celebrities and supermodels. Jaime clasped my hand as we elbowed our way through the crowd. His grip was firm, warm, and powerful.

"Gloria!" shouted out several paparazzi, blinding me with their flashes as they snapped my photo. I plastered a big fake smile on my face. God, did I hate this part of the job. Only Kevin knew I was actually rather shy. And that I harbored deep insecurities—leftovers from my past—beneath my powerhouse façade.

Jaime protectively ushered me through the mayhem. He wrapped his strong, manly arm around me, shielding me as I bowed my head. I hoped a photo of the two of us together wouldn't appear tomorrow on Page Six of the *New York Post*. I took a calming breath. There were way more intriguing people than me to feature. Like Kim Kardashian, who I'm sure would be here with her entourage or Justin Bieber who was also on the VIP list. Not to mention all the Gloria's Secret supermodels.

Inside the vast, three-story nightclub, loud, pulsating music blasted while candy-colored lights bounced off a giant disco ball. On the flat screen TV above the U-shaped bar, the Gloria's Secret Fashion Show was playing; it looked even more dazzling on television. I felt confident the ratings would be sensational.

The place was packed. Beautiful body after body was draped everywhere. Over lounges. Over the bar. Over each other. The smell of marijuana was thick in the air. Kevin found me quickly and ushered me away from Jaime to meet some of the VIPs. From the corner of my eye, I saw Jaime mingling in the crowd. He was turning heads, and before long, a dozen gorgeous supermodel types were fawning all over him. I recognized several of them from our fashion show. Former Jaime Zander fucks?

"Glorious, you look faa-bu-lous!" crooned Kevin, diverting my attention and unfounded jealousy away from Jaime.

"You look great too." True to himself, he was back to being outrageous. He was wearing an open white peasant shirt over Gloria's Secret leopard-patterned leggings and combat boots. Kev could one-up Marc Jacobs any day.

"No one can stop talking about the show. And we're killing it in the ratings!"

"Thanks to you." My eyes lit up, though I was feeling a little claustrophobic in this dark, frenetic environment.

He gave me a signature peck on both cheeks. "No, it's all you. Your dream. Your vision. I just make it happen."

Kev and I were a great team. He always made things happen—even the one thing we both wanted to forget. We had been through thick and thin. If we could survive our abusive childhoods and the unthinkable crime we'd committed together, we could survive anything.

He took me by the hand and swept me away "Come on, I want you to meet some of the VIPs. Actually, they want to meet you."

I stole a glance backward and my stomach twisted. Jaime was now chatting with Vivien. They seemed to be having a very intimate conversation. Jaime was hanging on her every word though his expression was impassive. There was no doubt in my mind that Vivien was coming on to him, with her pouts, hair flicks, and hip thrusts. She placed her hands on Jaime's shoulders and whispered into his ear. Jaime's eyes grew wide and then a faint smile played on his face. Before either of them could catch my gaze, I turned away and let Kevin lead me deeper into the crowd.

He introduced me to several VIPs that included top models, recording artists, and everyone's favorite reality TV stars. While I was cordially smiley-faced with all of them, my mind was focused on Jaime and Vivien. What was with them? My eyes searched the pulsing crowd, but I could no longer find them. Had Jaime left with her? My mental ramblings came to a halt when Kevin told me that he had to split and get the charity auction for Rihanna's diamond-studded bra and thong started. I was not standing alone for long.

"Gloria, lovely to see you." The cold, affected

drawl was unmistakable. Victor Holden, Vivien's father. My multi-billionaire biggest shareholder and Chairman of the Board.

He cupped his hands on my bare shoulders. His fingers, as usual, were as icy as his voice. With a shiver that shimmied down my spine, I spun around to face him.

Victor was in his mid fifties though his fit body and handsome face made him look at least ten years younger. He was a tall, lean, debonair man with slicked back salt and pepper hair, a permanent tan, and elegant features that included piercing steel gray eyes and an aquiline nose. Wearing an expensive tweed jacket, open-button dress shirt, and well-cut gabardine trousers, he exuded old money. A shrewd businessman, he was known for making vulnerable companies his prey. Many on Wall Street called him "The Vulture."

His eyes roamed down my body, lingering on places they had no right to be. But he felt he had the right to claim. He was always hitting on me. I was his prey too. I inwardly shuddered as he planted a wet kiss on each cheek.

"Well done today, darling. I'm sure the show will drive first quarter sales. Our shareholders will be pleased."

"Thank you, Victor." I hated when he called me "darling." The less I said to him the better. I always tried to keep it to dollars and cents.

"Why don't we celebrate with a dance?"

The last thing I wanted to do was dance with him. He moved uncomfortably close to me. The rancid smell of cigarettes mixed with alcohol on his breath assaulted my senses. He squeezed my jaw.

"Don't disappoint me, Gloria." He squeezed my jaw tighter.

"Please, Victor, you're hurting me." I jerked away. My pashmina shawl fell off my shoulders to the floor. Before I could bend down to pick it up, it was back on me, draped perfectly over my dress. I instantly recognized the scent of my hero. Jaime!

"Sorry, she's with me," he growled, wrenching me away from Victor. Their eyes clashed, the air between them thick with tension and animosity. Unspoken words flew between them. Victor's eyes narrowed into sharp slivers of glass as Jaime led me deeper into the crowd. As we neared the bar, I stole a glance back at Victor. He stood there motionless, his glacial eyes fixed on me. It was not the look of defeat but rather that of a man who wouldn't take "no" for answer. He frightened me.

"Do you know who that was?" I asked Jaime.

"A fucking asshole." His face hardened.

"Do you know he's the Chairman of—"

"Yeah, I know," he said, cutting me off. "I don't give a flying fuck."

His contempt for Victor shocked and enthralled me. "He could get in the way of you winning the Gloria's Secret account."

His jaw stiffened. "He won't." It softened. "Do you want a drink?"

"I'd love one," a female voice responded. Slinking up to us was Victor's daughter, Vivien, dressed to the nines in a fuchsia strapless bandage dress that hugged her curves and pushed up her D-cup boobs. Matching platform stilettos completed her ensemble. She flung back her loose ebony hair with a shake of her head, and gave Jaime a wide toothy predatory smile.

"Later," Jaime said coolly.

Vivien's face took on the expression of a miffed spoiled little rich girl who was used to getting anything she wanted. She glowered at me as she sauntered off. My face didn't move a muscle. *Bitch!*

"So where were we?" asked Jaime, his tone now sexy and seductive.

"Um, uh, a drink," I stammered. Drinking at business events was against my rules, but I sure could use one.

"What would you like?"

"A vodka martini with extra olives."

"Don't move." He strode over to the bar and returned quickly with two martinis, one for me, one for him.

"Thanks." As I put the cold, velvety liquid to my lips, the pulsating music came to a sudden halt. The auction for Rihanna's diamond-studded bra and thong had begun. All eyes, including Jaime's and mine, were riveted on the wiry auctioneer standing behind a podium at the front of the club. The items were displayed on a curvaceous mannequin to his right.

The bidding opened at $100,000. It quickly escalated to $500,000. My heart was palpitating. While I was seriously amazed that someone would pay so much money for a set of underwear (Okay, they were diamond-studded and Rihanna-strutted), I was thrilled because all the proceeds would go to Girls Like Us, the charitable organization I had started to help underprivileged and troubled teen girls pursue their dreams. Like me.

At $900,000, a new bidder stepped in. I recognized the icy voice immediately. Victor!

"I have $900,000. Do I hear one million dollars for these treasures?" shouted the enthusiastic auctioneer.

Dead silence. Everyone in the room held their breath.

"One million dollars."

I gasped. Jaime Zander had just shouted out that exorbitant figure. I shot him a wide-eyed look. A smug smile crossed his face. What the hell was he doing?

"One million dollars to the man with the gorgeous blonde."

I cringed. His smile widened.

"Do I hear one million five hundred thousand dollars?"

"Over here," chimed in Victor hastily. I turned my head, and my eyes met his. They burnt with fire and desire.

The auctioneer beamed behind his podium. "One point five million dollars. Do I hear any more bids?"

Silence again. I glanced again at Victor. He shot me a smarmy smile. The tension in the air was thick.

The auctioneer: "Going once...Going twice...Fair warning...Going down at..."

"Two million dollars!"

Jaime again! He raised his martini glass high in the air to confirm the bid. What the fuck? I gasped so loudly I was embarrassed. Fortunately, the din of the crowd's collective gasp drowned it out.

The auctioneer grinned. "It's back to the gentleman with the gorgeous blonde. Do I hear anything further?"

I eyed Victor once more. He was quietly fuming. I'd seen that sinister expression on his face before when he couldn't get what he wanted—especially at the price he was willing to pay.

The auctioneer slowly raised his hammer. "Going once." Silence. "Going twice." Silence. "Going... going...GONE!" He slammed his hammer down on the podium. "Sold for two million dollars to the gentleman with the gorgeous blonde! Congratulations, sir!"

Raucous applause and cheers broke out. The loud disco music started up again. The crowd began to dance wildly. The party was now just getting started. But I stood motionless in shock.

"Aren't you going to congratulate me, Gloria?" Jaime asked, catapulting me into the moment.

"Why did you buy the Rihanna undergarments? They cost a fortune."

"Because I could afford to. And the money's going to a good cause." He winked at me as he punctuated the words "good cause."

Smartass! "So, you think by impressing me with your money and audacity you'll win the Gloria's Secret account?" I countered, my voice testy.

His lips curled up into that sexy smile. "No. I'll win your account with my creativity and agility."

Arrogant asshole! But there was no denying that his words made me flush. Before I could utter a sound, he tugged at my braid.

"Dance with me, Gloria!" An order. Setting his half-finished martini onto a nearby cocktail table, he whisked me into his sculpted arms, drawing me tight against him. The dance music was pounding, and so was my heart...along with the wet bundle of nerves between my inner thighs. Against my silk dress, I could feel the rippled muscles of his chest and the rigid mound between his thighs. He pressed his arousal harder against me as he gyrated his hips against mine. I was as stiff as a board.

"Relax, Gloria," he commanded. "Trust me."

He splayed his long fingers on my jutting hipbones, rotating my hips to follow his. I chugged my martini, and as the velvety liquid coursed through my bloodstream, I felt myself loosening up. Soon I was rhythmically moving with him as if we'd danced together forever. His undulating movements were fluid, sensual, and controlling. Boy, did Mr. Agility know how to move!

A waiter passed by with a tray full of cocktails. Plunking my depleted martini glass on the tray, I grabbed another drink, not knowing what it was. I polished it off in two gulps, in time enough to return the emptied glass back onto the tray. I reached for one more. Jaime gripped my wrist forcefully, holding it back.

"Careful, Gloria." Jaime's voice whirled in my ear as the room started spinning around me. Was this some kind of special effect? My favorite new song, "Blurred Lines," began to play. I was totally into it, singing along at the top of my lungs.

"Do you think I'm a good girl?" I asked Jaime, slurring each word.

"Come on, let's get of here." Jaime's voice took on urgency.

"No!" I protested. "I just want to dance." I looped my arms around his neck, brushing them along his silky tousled hair, and glued my forehead to his. My hot breath caught his, and I started to move wildly, bumping every part of me against his rock-hard body. My hips. My butt. My boobs. Without losing physical contact, I pulled off my shoes.

"Don't need these!" I chirped and tossed them deep into the crowd.

"Let's go. Now!" ordered Jaime.

Before I could protest again, Jaime yanked my arms off his neck, grabbed a hand, and dragged me through the crowd. Dazed and dizzy, I tottered behind him, barely managing to keep up with him.

I passed by Vivien and waved at her. She fired me a scathing look. I was confused. Everything was a whirling blur.

Finally, we were outside. The cool, crisp air enveloped me but did little to bring me to my senses. The world, which revolved around the devastatingly handsome Jaime Zander, was still spinning out of control. I felt myself swaying. Thank goodness, this gorgeous hunk of manliness was holding me up, his muscled arm clamped around my waist. He slipped his spare hand into his jeans pocket and pulled out his cell phone. He fingered the touch-key screen and I heard him mumble, "Orson, I need the car brought around to the entrance of the club immediately."

"How do you feel?" Jaime asked upon ending the call. His voice was tender.

"Like shit," I murmured. Nausea had settled in. Bile was rising to my chest. *Oh God, please don't let me throw up in front of him! Please! NO!*

The next thing I knew, Mr. Zander was scooping me up in his arms and loading me into the back seat of his Rover. He cradled me in his lap, his hard length pressing into my backside, and let me lean my head against his chest. Though his chest was pure steel, the softness of his cotton tee was comforting.

"I'm sorry," I rasped, barely able to get out the words as I fought back nausea.

"Don't be." He smoothed my hair along my scalp and then twisted my long platinum braid around his fingers.

"Rihanna's underwear!" I mumbled, the events of the night whirling around in my head.

"Don't worry." He pressed his warm lips against my forehead. Even in my drunken stupor, his touch zapped every fiber of my being.

I gazed up at him. Gah! There were two of him! Double the gorgeousness. "Do you have an identical twin?" I slurred.

"Ah, my Gloria." He chuckled. "You'll soon find out that I'm a one and only. Just like you. "

The muffled sound of late night traffic of the city that never sleeps drifted into my ears. Somewhere during the ride back to the hotel, everything faded to black.

Chapter 5

J AIME ZANDER WAS POUNDING INTO me. His thick pulsing cock going to the hilt. Hitting my magic spot again and again. Driving me insanely wild. I moaned with ecstasy and dug my nails into his flesh. He was on top of me, the weight and strength of him holding me prisoner.

"Let go, Gloria. Come for me," he barked, his hot breath in my mouth. He grinded faster and deeper, each stroke bringing me closer to the edge. I clung onto his biceps as the muscles of my core began to convulse. Inside my body, a spiraling tornado was taking everything in its wake. My head was ringing, spinning out of control.

The loud ringing wouldn't stop. Reality set in, and I realized it was my room phone. It stopped before I could answer it.

Drenched in sweat, I pried my eyes open, one at a time, and after blinking several times, took in my surroundings. I was back at the hotel...in my bed. My head was pounding and my tongue was stuck to my parched, foul-tasting palate. It must be morning; a ray of sunshine beamed through the blackout curtains. I had kicked off the fluffy duvet sometime during the night. Splayed on the bed, I was draped in a sexy lavender lace Gloria's Secret baby doll with matching bikinis.

Wait! How did I get back here? What happened to my little black dress? My lingerie? My shoes? The events of last night spun around in my head. Slowly, the fuzziness gave way to clarity. Fuck! I got drunk last night! I vaguely remembered Jaime Zander escorting me out of the club and lifting me into his SUV. And after that, I couldn't remember a damn thing. Oh, God! I must have passed out.

My breath caught in my throat. Had that cocky asshole brought me up to my room and undressed me? My mind raced; my heart raced. Holy, holy shit! Had he taken advantage of me and fucked me? Was that a dream or was that for real? A wave of panic swept over me.

The phone on my nightstand rang again. This time I managed to reach for it with an outstretched arm. It was Nigel, my driver.

"Good morning, Miss Long," he chimed, his voice chipper. "I shall be waiting for you at the entrance of the hotel at ten a.m. as you requested."

My brain still in lockdown, it took me a long moment to remember what I was doing today. *Gloria to brain. Come in now.* Yes. I was going to visit my beloved mentor, Madame Paulette. Thank goodness, Nigel had called because I hadn't arranged for my customary wake-up call. Raising myself to a sitting position, I freed my tongue from my dry as cardboard palate.

"Thank you, Nigel." And then I remembered something else. "A boy or girl?"

"A six pound four ounce baby girl!" exclaimed Nigel on the other end. "Her name is Annabelle."

"That's wonderful, Nigel!" Despite my sorry state, a smile spread across my face. "Congratulations! I'll see you soon."

After returning the phone to its cradle, I made myself a mental note: Make sure the gift is sent today. I had already purchased an expensive stroller along with a travel bag full of baby care necessities. It gave me pleasure knowing that Nigel's daughter would appreciate everything. After my visit to Madame Paulette, I was also going to give him the rest of the day off so that he could spend it with his daughter and new grandchild.

The mental diversion was short lived. My mind jumped back to Jaime Zander. A shudder rippled through me. I'd made a total fool of myself and now, I was fucked—in maybe more ways than one. How could I ever face him again?

I picked up the phone once more and dialed room service. I ordered a large pot of coffee—something I desperately needed if I was going to make it through the day. At least, I had some time to figure out how I was going to handle Jaime. His pitch meeting wasn't until late afternoon tomorrow. Getting out of the city might give me some clarity.

My visit to Madame Paulette was something I looked forward to as much as I dreaded. It would probably be the last time I saw her. She was, along with Kevin, the most important person in my life. With a heavy heart and hangover from hell, I dragged myself out of bed and staggered to the bathroom.

I glimpsed myself in the bathroom mirror. My reflection startled me. I looked as bad as I felt. My skin was greenish and my eyes red. Waves of nausea were still rolling through me. I brushed my teeth to freshen my stale breath and popped a couple of much needed Advils into my mouth. I desperately needed a shower. As I lifted my baby doll top over my head, the alluring scent of Gloria's Secret men's cologne assailed my nostrils. I instantly buried my nose in the silky fabric. The intoxicating scent of him was all over it. My stomach knotted. Oh God, had he? Panicky, I yanked off the matching bottoms. Scrunching them in my hand, I checked my body for more evidence. There were no signs of bruising, and neither my breasts nor my privates were sore or engorged. I took a whiff of the bikinis—oh no, the distinct scent of him again! Yet, there was no trace of any residue on the crotch. I impulsively rubbed my cleft and put my wet fingers to my nose. The distinct sweet smell was definitely all mine, but I still couldn't be sure. Maybe he washed off all the evidence. Damn him! Damn me for losing control!

The hot, pulsing shower was revitalizing. I arched my head back with eyes squeezed shut and let the jets of water spray my face while I lathered up my body with the fragrant soap. Nothing felt out of the ordinary except the lingering nauseous feeling. Turning off the faucet, I stepped out of the shower and wrapped a giant bath towel around me. I studied myself in the bathroom mirror. I looked better than I'd thought I would. The hot shower had done its magic. My porcelain skin was glowing, and there was only a trace of broken capillaries in my duo-colored eyes. I re-braided my long blond wet hair and applied a dollop of lip-gloss. I wanted to look groomed for Madame Paulette. Appearance was important to her.

Returning to the bedroom, I noticed for the first time that my little black dress and lingerie from last night were missing. And where the hell were my shoes? Again the question: Who the hell took them off me? I searched the drawers, looked under the bed, and scanned the closet. *Gone. Gone. Gone.* I glanced at the alarm clock on the night table. It was already nine forty-five. Nigel would be here soon to take me to Connecticut. Hastily, I donned a lacy gray bra and bikini set, matching garter and sheer gray silk hose. A lady-like A-line gray dress and pewter pumps followed. I always matched the color of my underwear to what I was wearing. It was something Madame Paulette had taught me to do. My life lessons from this incredible woman were many and meaningful. Sadly, she would soon be gone.

The coffee still hadn't arrived. As much as I craved a major dose of caffeine, I couldn't wait for it. Grabbing my coat, purse, and a canvas bag full of goodies that I knew Madame Paulette would adore, I skirted out of the room and headed to the elevators.

"Hey, wait up!"

That deep, sexy voice. Fuck! It was him! Jaime Zander. What the hell was he doing here?

Bristling, I kept marching without a single turn of my head. I could hear him jogging down the corridor. He caught up to me, and we stood side by side waiting for the lift. Staring straight ahead, I refused to look at him. Not even a little glimpse.

Unlike yesterday, the elevator took its time arriving. In fact, it felt like an eternity. Maybe it was stuck somewhere—explaining why my coffee had never arrived. My stomach tightened and I was losing patience. He started whistling—"Gloria" of all songs. *Bastard!* He was trying to distract me and get my attention.

"Stop that!"

"You don't like my whistling?"

"I don't like you." And then it just came flying out. "Did you fuck me last night?"

"Gloria, I would never take advantage of you in that state. In case you don't remember, I carried you up to your room and then you threw up all over yourself."

Holy crap! Mortification raced through me. I kept facing the elevator, too embarrassed to look him in the face.

"There's nothing to be embarrassed about. You're just not used to losing control."

I never lost control! *Never!* What had this man done to me?

"By the way, I gave your dress and undergarments to the valet for cleaning. They should be back in your room by five. Unfortunately, someone else may be wearing your shoes. You may not recall this, but you took them off and tossed them while you were dancing with me."

I couldn't care less now about my eight hundred dollar designer shoes. Every muscle in my body clenched. The reality of him undressing me and seeing me naked consumed me.

"Don't be ashamed. You have a beautiful body.

While taking off your vomit-coated dress was not exactly something I enjoyed, peeling off your silky stockings from those long smooth legs and tearing off that sexy bra and garter were quite a treat."

I felt my cheeks flare. In fact, my whole body was heating up. *Come on, elevator. Get here already.* His words got in the way.

"Your breasts should be among the wonders of the world, and your perfectly preened pussy was a sight to behold. I wouldn't mind getting a taste of it some time. When was the last time you got laid?"

"None of your damn business!"

"That's what I thought."

He was infuriating me. What's more, he was setting every fiber of my being on fire, especially the area between my thighs. Where the hell was the elevator? I had to get away from him. Finally, a car arrived. As soon as the doors slid opened, I stomped into it. I slammed my palm against the "L" button, but the doors wouldn't close. That's because the asshole was leaning against one, his arms and legs seductively crossed.

For the first time this morning, he was in full view. All six foot three of his manly gorgeousness. Today, he was wearing a fringed tan suede jacket with tight faded blue jeans that hung low on his narrow hips, a plaid flannel shirt that exposed his chiseled pecs...and cowboy boots! Mr. Urban Cowboy! God, he looked sexy! Right out of *GQ!* And on top of all that, his hair had that perfectly tousled, just-fucked look going on.

An unnerving thought shot into my head. Did he fuck someone else after he left me? A beautiful supermodel? Vivien? Maybe he kept a room at this hotel as a fuck pad. Lots of successful men did that kind of thing.

My eyes narrowed. "Can you please either leave or get in?"

That cocky half-smile curled on his lips. "I just want to get a good look at you." His sexy denim blues gave me the once-over. "You look lovely, Gloria."

I grimaced. "It's Ms. Long."

"You're not very polite, *Ms.* Long."

"Thank you," I grumbled. *Screw you!*

"That's better." With a thrust of his hips, he strode into the elevator and stood right next to me. The doors closed instantly, and we began our high-speed descent. I inhaled his intoxicating scent but kept my eyes focused straight ahead.

He broke the silence. "Oh, by the way, did you like the negligee I picked out for you?"

My face flushed crimson and my stomach muscles scrunched. In my mind's eye, I could just see the wicked grin on his face.

"It sufficed," I murmured through gritted teeth. Actually, the lacy lavender peek-a-boo set from our "Sweet Temptations" baby doll collection was one of my favorites.

"I hope you'll be a little more enthusiastic about my pitch." His voice dripped with sarcasm.

I pressed my lips together and said nothing. To my relief, he remained silent for the rest of the ride. We reached the lobby in no time, and the elevator doors re-opened. As I moved to dash out, he fisted my braid, holding me back. The nerve of him! Fuming, I turned on my heels to face him. My eyes met his equally intense gaze.

"Are you visiting another ad agency today?" he asked. "There's really no need to."

His presumptuousness got under my skin. Should I tell him that I was visiting a dozen more, just to make him think that he had a lot of competition?

"No," I finally said.

"Good." With a satisfied smile, he let go of my hair and accompanied me to the hotel entrance, keeping up with my slower than normal pace. There was no physical contact between us. Whatsoever.

It was another beautiful New York City winter day. Sunny and not too cold. The usual array of cabs and limos crowded the driveway.

"Do you want to grab breakfast with me?" he asked.

God, a coffee would be so good. Even if I had to put up with the pompous asshole. I glanced down at my watch. Ten a.m. "I can't. My driver will be here momentarily."

"What about lunch?"

"I'm visiting someone out of town."

"Oh, a boyfriend?"

"Yes!" I shouted the word and didn't know why I lied.

"Happy Valentine's Day!" He winked.

My jaw clenched. "Same to you."

Thankfully, before Mr. Nosy and Infuriating could probe further, Nigel pulled up to the curb.

Wearing a warm smile, he jumped out of the town car and opened the back passenger door. As I slid into the car, Jaime Zander never took his contemplative eyes off me. His lips twisted again into that maddening grin as the car rolled away. Fuck! I bet he saw right though my white lie...the tinted windows...and my coat.

Chapter 6

THE DRIVE ALONG THE SCENIC Merritt Parkway to Connecticut was relaxing. I alternated between catching up on e-mails and gazing out the window. A fine layer of snow dusted the lawns of residences we passed by. Snow was something I rarely saw living in Los Angeles.

I would be lying if I said I didn't think about Jaime Zander. I couldn't get him out of my head. He was having an effect on me like no other man had before. I'd never met a man who could reduce me to a nervous wreck with the just wink of an eye. Make me feel so totally out of control. It scared me. Big-decision-maker-me didn't know how to handle it. Why the hell didn't I just tell him to fuck off? And forget about the pitch for my business? Walk away from him while I had the chance? The truth: He had gotten under my skin. I was undeniably drawn to him—both to his sexy good looks and his challenging personality. He was as tempting as he was toxic. Even now, just thinking about him, I was quivering. I sat back against the soft leather seat, glad to be away from him.

To get my mind off him, I went back to checking my e-mails. I opened Kevin's first; there were several. The first one brought a big smile to my face.

Happy Valentine's Day, Glorious!
XOXO —Kev

I e-mailed him right back.

MWAH! Same to you!

Kevin had been my one and only Valentine forever. Neither of us had ever had much luck in the love department. But we had each other. Hopefully, tonight we could celebrate together although we hadn't made any firm plans. Our traditional pity party for two could be on the agenda.

Waiting for his reply, I read the rest of his e-mails. All great news. The televised broadcast of the Gloria's Secret Fashion Show had rocked in the ratings, and sales were at record levels at our stores worldwide. Yes, women were flocking to Gloria's Secret last minute to buy seductive lingerie and sleepwear for the romantic Valentine's night ahead. And they were standing in line with men, who were clutching replacement pieces for those that might get torn off after a candlelit dinner. I found it bitterly ironic that I sold love and sex but was never on the receiving end. Always on this day, my elation over sales was met with a pang of sadness. My mind jumped again to Jaime Zander. I bet he had a hot date tonight; women were all over him; I saw it with my own eyes. With a heavy heart, I eagerly awaited an e-mail from Kevin to cheer me up.

An hour and a half into the drive, we exited the parkway and followed a rural, wooded road to the retirement home where Madame Paulette was residing. A magnificent gated estate soon came into view. Once the Normandy-styled mansion of one of America's great oil barons, it was now the Cadbury House for Assisted Living. What I'd read about it had put my mind at ease. The pedigreed staff was attentive, the surroundings luxurious, and the cuisine delicious—prepared by a French chef. I was thrilled that I was able to afford to place my beloved Paulette here for her final years. Even though I had made her a wealthy woman with Gloria's Secret stock, there was no way I could let her pay for her care. I owed her everything.

The call I had received from the head caretaker just before I'd left for New York had been unsettling. In fact, it had brought tears to my eyes. Madame Paulette's health was failing rapidly, and it was unlikely she'd make it to the summer. Even if I didn't have business in New York, I would have hopped the corporate jet and come East to visit her. She meant the world to me. She was my mentor, my role model, and the mother I never had. Upon learning about her numbered days, I vowed I would confess the secret I had harbored my entire adult life. She needed to know. I needed to tell.

Standing in the elegantly appointed entrance with her bag of goodies in hand, I anxiously awaited for someone to show me to her room. Nurse Perez, a jovial, curly-haired buxom woman, appeared in no time and escorted me up a magnificent winding marble staircase to the second floor. "We all love

Paulette," she said as I trailed close behind her. What was there not to love? She was an extraordinary human being who would be sorely missed.

Madame's suite was located at the end of the corridor. Her door was wide open. She gasped when she saw me. I hadn't told her I was coming. It was a surprise.

"*Ma chérie!*" she exclaimed. Her voice was deeper and raspier than ever. Over the course of her long life, she had smoked way too many French cigarettes and drunk way too many glasses of wine.

Clad in an elegant lace-trimmed white nightgown, she was propped up in a luxurious down-covered bed against a half a dozen plump pillows. Despite her age—she must have been close to ninety though she'd never admit to it—she was as beautiful to me as ever. Her strong-featured face seemed to be wrinkle-resistant, and her hair, now a shimmering silver, was tied back as usual in a regal chignon. Even in her old age, she epitomized grace and style.

Fighting back tears, I sprinted over to her. We exchanged lots of cheek-to-cheek kisses.

"It *eez* so good to see you," she said as I plunked down in armchair next to her bed.

"I'm in New York on a business trip." There was no way I was going to divulge the real reason behind my visit. "I've brought you all your favorite magazines."

I handed her the bag full of fashion magazines. Her face lit up as she removed the contents, one by one. *"Mes favorites!"* She examined the cover of a *Vogue* featuring Jennifer Lopez. "But why do *les américains* always put those Hollywood *célébrités* on the cover?"

She made me laugh when I wanted to cry. Even our Gloria's Secret catalogue now featured celebrities like J-Lo on the cover. The bottom line: celebrities moved merchandise.

As she flipped through some of the magazines, we spent time chitchatting, catching up. She complained about the food—way too *nouveau* for her taste. And why couldn't she have more than one glass of wine? I, in turn, told her about how well Gloria's Secret was doing.

"Beezness shmeezness," she muttered. "Are you in love, *ma chérie?*"

I flushed. Jaime Zander's gorgeous face unexpectedly flashed into my head. I tried my damnedest to make it go away. No luck.

"No," I replied.

Madame Paulette studied my face with her intense cappuccino eyes. *"Ma chérie,* you cannot fool me. Your glow *geeves* it away." Signaling with her index finger for me to move in closer to her, she said, "You must tell me everything about *zee* new boyfriend."

"He's not my boyfriend," I protested as I slid my chair up to her bed railing.

"What *eez* his name?"

"Jaime."

"How do you spell that?"

"J-A-I-M-E."

"Ah, like *'J'aime.'* In French, that means, 'I love.'"

Of course. I suddenly remembered Madame Paulette telling me *"Je t'aime beaucoup." I love you very much*...when I thought love had abandoned me.

"So, *ma chérie,* are you in love with him?"

In love? I blushed. "I just met him."

"AH! *Zee* best! Love at first sight."

I still couldn't get Jaime Zander's beautiful face out my head. My heart pattered. No, it was not possible.

A melancholic smile flickered on Madame Paulette's face. "Always remember, *ma chérie,* it *eez* better to have loved and lost than never to have loved at all."

I wondered—had Madame Paulette ever been in love? While she always referred to herself as Madame, she had never mentioned a spouse, and I'd never been comfortable asking about her love life or her past. I'd always had a hunch, however, that she had once been married and had tragically lost the great love of her life. Once a year, on the eve of the Jewish holiday, Yom Kippur, the Day of Remembrance, she lit a candle that burned for twenty-four hours. I had asked her about the significance of the candle, and she had told me it was to commemorate someone special. While she always had dashing suitors who brought her flowers or French bonbons, she dismissed them all with a roll of her eyes. Whoever she had once loved couldn't be replaced.

A cheery Nurse Perez entered the room, carrying a tray. "Your lunch, Madame."

"Merci," growled Madame Paulette.

Smiling, Nurse Perez placed the bed tray over her lap, setting out the cutlery and linens. "Bon appétit," she said before parting.

"Bon appétit," Madame Paulette mock-mimicked. She was as feisty and as brutally honest as ever.

"This *eez* French TV dinner," she grumbled, reluctantly digging a fork into the mishmash of food. *"Gar-bahge!"*

Stifling a laugh, I reached into my large designer purse. "I've brought you something else." I handed her a medium-sized, gold-foiled box that was sealed with a wide red ribbon. She opened it with her still long and elegant fingers. The fingers that had adjusted thousands upon thousands of bra straps to bring out the best in women.

Her face lit up. "Ah! Bonbons. *Mes favorites!"*

I pecked her cheek. "Happy Valentine's Day!"

"Ah, *zee* day of love. So silly! Every day should be a day of love."

A bittersweet smile tickled my lips. I was going to miss Madame's words of wisdom.

She popped one of the rich chocolate treats into her mouth and savored it. *"Merci beaucoup, ma chérie.* You must have one."

I helped myself to one of the chocolates and let it melt in my mouth. It was pure deliciousness. After swallowing the last morsel, the sweet taste of the dark chocolate dissolved into the bitter taste of dark memories. It was time.

"Madame," I said hesitantly. "I must tell you something."

"What *eez* it, *ma chérie?* There *eez* sadness in your eyes."

My mind flashed back fifteen years. Kevin and I were both teenagers —sixteen-year-olds who had run away from our small rural upstate New York town. He to escape the brutal beatings of his father, a macho local sheriff, who had no tolerance for his son's homosexuality, and I to escape the wrath I endured as the daughter of the neighborhood crack whore. "Who's your daddy?" the kids at school would taunt when I was a skinny pig-tailed youngster. For all I knew, it could be any one of their fathers. My narcissistic mother, never there for me (I was an unwanted accident discovered too late to be aborted), slept with them all to indulge her sick addictions. Then, at fifteen, late-bloomer me sprouted five inches, and my flat-as-a-board breasts morphed into spheres. Boys would grab at me, try to pull my pants down, and call me names like slut, whore, and skank. They equated me with my mother, who I was not.

Kevin was always there to protect me. He'd learned Tai Kwan Do to protect himself from his own share of bullies and could send one of my molesters to his knees with a roundhouse kick. But this was not the life we wanted, so we decided to run away together. To find a new life in a big city like New York where we could fit in or disappear.

Kevin stole a gun from his father along with a few hundred dollars, which he kept locked in a safe. The gun and the money were all we had to start off on our new life together. We managed to hitch our way to New York City where we ended up in Brooklyn in the heart of Brighton Beach. Kevin charmed his way into securing a small one-bedroom rental apartment and used the money to buy some flea-market furnishings. We both needed to find work fast. Kevin, who had a flair for words, found a position teaching English to the children of neighborhood Russian immigrants, and I landed a sales job at a local lingerie store, Madame Paulette's.

I'd been combing the busy streets for work for hours when I came upon the big "Sales Help Wanted" sign in the storefront window. I'll never forget walking into her shop. With Edith Piaf's "La Vie en Rose" playing in the background, I took in all the luxurious silk and lace lingerie that Madame Paulette imported from Paris. Tables of delicate, perfectly folded brassieres, panties, and garters mingled with carefully organized racks of beautiful slips, negligees, and robes. There was also a carousel filled with package after package of fine silk stockings. Standing erect behind the cash register, the petite but chic Madame Paulette was dressed in her signature gray A-line skirt and perfectly pressed white blouse and drinking a glass of red wine. I introduced myself and told her I was interested in the sales position. She gave me the once-over and nodded approvingly. In her deep raspy voice, she said, "*Ma chérie, zee* shape of a woman's breasts lies in *zee* straps. Let me see if you know how to adjust one."

Leaving her wine behind, she led me to a small dressing room in the rear of the store where a well-heeled buxom woman was trying on numerous bras. Madame Paulette beheld the half-naked woman in her ill-fitting lacy bra and shook her head. "Ah, *non, non, non.* It *eez* all wrong for you." Sorting through the pile of bras strewn on a petite gold-leafed chair, she found another and handed it to her. "Please put on *zees* one, and *mademoiselle* will adjust it." With a nod of her chin, she looked my way.

The stocky woman nervously slipped on the big-cupped bra, front to back, and I hastily hooked it. Madame Paulette shot me a pleased smile. I surveyed the customer in the bra; the bra had potential but was not fitting her quite right. With nimble fingers, I tightened both straps, lifting up her generous boobs. I had learned how to put on a bra from watching my mother prepare for her "dates." At least the crack whore had been good for something. And being a difficult fit myself with my full C-cup breasts, which I'd inherited from her, I was quite an expert on making bras fit, though mine were the cheap cotton K-Mart variety.

"Now bend over and wiggle your breasts into the cups." I said after I finished adjusting the straps.

The woman did as asked and then stood up. She looked at herself in the floor length mirror, and her face lit up. The lacy, underwire bra fit her perfectly and did wonders for her saggy boobs. "I'll take it and two more just like it!"

"*Superbe!*" Madame Paulette beamed. "I will have my *new* assistant wrap *zeem* up."

My heart broke into a happy dance. I had landed the job as Madame Paulette's sales assistant. Always good with my hands, I wrapped up the bras in beautiful layers of delicate, scented tissue paper. The ecstatic customer couldn't wait to hand over a crisp hundred-dollar bill for the three bras.

From that day on, I worked from ten to six every day except Saturdays when Madame Paulette, who I learned was Jewish and from Paris, took a day off to observe Shabbat. Despite her diminutive size, she was an incredible, bigger than life woman who understood people, understood life, and understood the basic need women had to look and feel beautiful under their clothes. She taught me about how to examine the quality of lace, how to tell the difference between nylon and silk stockings, how to take a woman's measurements, how to make an alluring window display, how to charm customers, and even how to handle gentlemen who were shopping for something sexy for their secret mistresses. "Life *eez* no fun without sex or wine," she would preach. Twice a year, she would go to Paris and handpick items for the boutique. Every day, she gave me a French lesson so that one day I would be prepared to go to Paris. "*Zee* French are so *difficiles*," she'd always complain in her charming accent.

The one thing I'd noticed while working at her store was the number of young women who stopped in on their lunch breaks or way home from work, allured by the beautiful display windows. Inside the shop, they lusted for the exquisite but exorbitant French lingerie that they, like me, couldn't afford. I was convinced there was a market for gorgeous, sexy underwear at a reasonable price. When I shared this thought with Madame Paulette, she shooed me away with a dismissive wave of her hand. "*Mon dieu!* I can sell nothing but *zee* best!"

I'd been working for her for a little over two years and had just turned eighteen when over a bottle of Bordeaux, which we shared every Friday evening to welcome Shabbat, Madame Paulette broke the news that she wanted to retire and was going to sell the business. My heart sank. There was no guarantee that the store would remain a lingerie shop or if I was promised a job. "Would you like to buy it, *ma chérie?*" she asked. After the shock died down, I told her I would love to, but there was no way I could come up with the twenty-five thousand dollar down payment. Madame Paulette was as disappointed as I was but needed the money for her retirement.

A potential buyer was in the picture—Boris Borofsky. He was a tough Russian gangster—a freakish pink-eyed albino—who wanted to buy the business for his idle, bottle-blond trophy wife, Ina. The latter took a strong disliking to me, and I knew if the deal went through, I'd be out of a job. I wanted the business so badly. I had visions for it and dreams! But with my meager wages and the cost of living in Brooklyn, I hadn't managed to save a penny.

Kevin, with his boyish good looks and winning personality, had gotten a job as the host of an underground "men's club" that happened to be owned by the obnoxious Russian pursuing Madame Paulette's business. He'd been able to save five thousand dollars and offered the cash to me.

"Kev, I can't take your money," I sobbed, touched by his offer. "Plus, I would need to come up with another twenty thousand."

"I have an idea," he said.

I listened without interruption as he explained his plan...to rob the club. He hated the abusive Russian more than I did. He was a cheap, foul-mouthed womanizer without an ounce of humanity. Moreover, he was a gay-basher who had threatened Kevin with both his job and life. Because many of his business deals involved drugs, prostitution, and human trafficking, he kept hoards of loose cash in a safe in the basement. A single security guard made regular deposits after hours.

A deep shudder ran through me as I flashed back to that terrible night. A night I wished I could forget but couldn't. The night of terror that scarred me forever, emotionally and physically. The vault...the alarm...the assault...the gun shots...the screaming... the pain...the blackness...the blood. My eyes grew watery.

"Madame, I did something terrible." A tear trickled down my cheek. "I hope you can forgive me." I recounted my crime with no detail spared. By the time I was done telling her the secret I'd hidden all these years, I was a blubbering mess.

She took my icy cold hands in her warm ones. "*Ma pauvre petite*, you are lucky to be alive."

Her reaction stunned me. I thought for sure she would condemn me. She tenderly brushed away my tears and continued.

"Do you know, *ma chérie,* the Russian came to my store looking for you?"

My tear-soaked eyes widened. "He did?"

"*Oui.* I knew there was something terribly wrong because you did not come to work or call in for several days. *En plus,* he was missing teeth, and there was a thick bandage on each cheek."

Kevin's bullet! It must have gone through one cheek and out the other. I faintly remembered hearing Boris curse as I lost consciousness in Kevin's arms.

Madame continued. "He was very angry but could barely move his mouth. He wanted to know your name. I made up a different name and told him that you no longer worked for me. Since I paid you in cash, there was no way for him to find out your real identity."

I was speechless. Unbeknownst to me all these years, Madame Paulette had helped save my life.

"I immediately called your apartment. That handsome young gentleman friend of yours luckily answered *zee* phone. I told him that I believed your life was in terrible danger and that you should get as far away from Brooklyn as possible. I offered him money, but he told me there was no need."

The hazy memory of a panicked Kevin telling me that Boris was after me flitted into my head. I was weak, still in bed, barely recovered from my gunshot wound. Kevin threw together a duffel bag full of basics, and two hours later, he was pushing me in a wheelchair through Kennedy Airport with the sack of money on my lap. I vaguely remembered him telling the suspicious security guard that the cash was for a much needed surgical procedure. Glib Kevin could talk his way through anything. Soon after, we were on a plane to Los Angeles on our way to safety.

A harsh cough from Madame Paulette brought me back to the moment. My heart was melting. She was both my mentor and savior. Blinking back tears, I wrapped my arms around her frail body and hugged her. "Madame, how can I ever thank you enough?"

"You must stop crying, *ma chérie.*" Her expression grew wistful. "We've all done terrible things we've regretted to survive."

My sobbing came to a halt. "What do you mean?"

"When I was a young woman, I slept with a Nazi

officer to save my family."

I gasped. Had she lived with this horrible secret her whole life?

"Had I not, we would have all been sent to a concentration camp."

I was speechless.

"*Alors, ma chérie,* you must forgive yourself. You have redeemed yourself and done many noble things with what came of it. I am proud of you."

I hugged her again. It was probably the last time we'd embrace.

She sighed against me. "I still wish you could have bought my *beezness.*"

Boris Borofsky had purchased it, but sadly, his incompetent wife ran it into the ground. It was now a Starbucks. The fate of Madame Paulette's boutique tugged at my heartstrings. If only things had worked out...but "what ifs" didn't matter anymore. I gently squeezed her hand.

Another caregiver stepped into the room. This time a handsome silver-haired doctor. "I'm afraid, Ms. Long, that Madame must take her nap now."

"Bah! Sleep *eez* for *zee* dead!" grumbled Madame Paulette after he left.

Her words at once amused and saddened me. The reality that she was going to die soon hit me hard. I held back more tears.

I gave her a final double-cheeked hug, and then we just held each other. Her frail bones warmed mine. When we finally broke away from each other, she wearily said, "*Ma chérie,* there *eez* something else I want to tell you." She paused while her eyes grew watery. "I had a husband. His name was Henri

Lévy. He died fighting for the Résistance. I want to be buried next to him." She ripped out a sheet of paper from the writing pad on her night table and scribbled something on it. "This *eez zee* name of *zee* cemetary," she said handing it to me. I folded up the sheet and placed it in my bag.

"*Oui,* Madame. I will take care of it." A fresh round of tears was verging.

She smiled contently and closed her eyes. Softly, she repeated what she'd said earlier. "Remember, *ma chérie*, that it *eez* better to have loved and lost than never to have loved at all."

I tiptoed out of the room with a less guilty conscience and the newfound knowledge that Madame Paulette had indeed known true love.

Chapter 7

T HE RIDE BACK TO THE city was uneventful. We were in counter-traffic and made excellent time. I thought about what Madame Paulette had told me... and Jaime Zander. I wondered if I would bump into him at the hotel or have to wait until tomorrow's pitch at his office. I pined for the former.

We got back to the hotel by four p.m. I headed straight to my room, caught up on some e-mails, took a short nap, and showered. As I towel dried myself, the room phone rang. My heart galloped. Could it be Jaime? Wrapping the towel around me, I sprinted to the phone. With a shaky hand, I picked up the receiver.

"Glorious."

It was Kevin.

"I'm sorry I haven't been in touch. I've been crazed all day with post-show interviews. I have to have dinner with some of the models and a network executive. Do you want to come along?"

After such an emotional afternoon, the last thing I wanted to do was have dinner at some pretentious restaurant with a bunch of bubblehead models and some fawning network guy.

"If it's okay, I'm going to pass, Kev. I'm beat." At some point, I wanted to tell him about my encounter with Madame Paulette, but this wasn't the time.

"It's Valentine's Day. Are you sure you're going to be okay?"

Kevin knew how downtrodden I got on this holiday. "Yeah. I'm going to order room service and curl up with some book boyfriend."

Kevin mock-sniffed. "But I'm your one and only Valentine."

I laughed. "Don't worry. You are. Have fun tonight!"

"Mwah! Happy Valentine's Day, Glorious. I love you."

"Love you back."

As I hung up the phone, a pang of sadness stabbed me. Book boyfriends were as close as I'd ever gotten to the real thing.

Though it was now only 5:30, I was ravenous. Other than the chocolate, I hadn't eaten a thing all day. My body was crying out for food. Maybe a good steak, a baked potato, and an iced tea. Definitely no alcohol after last night's binge, the effects of which still lingered a little.

As I was about to reach for the phone, it rang again. I picked it up on the second ring.

"Have you had dinner yet?"

Jaime! I sucked in a gulp of air. "Don't you have a hot Valentine's date?"

"No. I don't do love."

"Neither do I."

"Then, come eat with me."

Silence.

"My suite is three doors down to the right."

Silence.

"We can talk business."

Silence.

"Just get your lovely ass over here."

Jaime's corner suite was triple the size of mine—a mini palace in the sky. Floor-to-ceiling windows wrapped around it and overlooked the sparkling city. The views were breathtaking.

The lights were dimmed, and scattered candles scented the air. He ushered me to a black leather couch and strode over to a built-in veneer cabinet in the corner. Putting on some soft jazz, he said, "Room service should be here any minute. I hope you don't mind that I've already ordered for both of us."

"Perfectly fine." I couldn't take my eyes off him. Casually dressed in charcoal sweats that hung low on his hips and a soft white tee—and barefoot— he looked freshly showered and sexy as hell. How could he always look this way? Having slipped back into the gray ensemble that I'd worn earlier in the day to keep things businesslike, I felt overdressed and uptight.

I surveyed his suite. While mine was decorated with mid-century reproductions, I got the sense that the furnishings in his were authentic and included pieces from Bauhaus, Charles Eames, and others. He had moreover personalized the spacious interior with a bold geometric patterned rug and colorful pillows that picked up the hues of the many intriguing abstract paintings scattered on the walls. They were similar in style to the ones in his office and all signed PAZ.

He crossed the room with his long-legged confident gait and sunk into a creamy leather armchair opposite me. My eyes roamed down his face and landed on his crotch. Holy shit! There was a tent between his thighs!

"Do you live here full time?" I asked, fumbling for conversation.

"Yeah."

Okay, so it wasn't a fuck pad, but it was still an odd living arrangement. Was it because he could fuck transient women and never have to see them again? I mentally slapped myself and asked, "Why do you live in a hotel?"

"It's convenient. I work long hours and travel a lot, so having all these amenities makes things easier."

I could understand that because I lived in a full maintenance high-rise building in Los Angeles that catered to my every whim—except room service.

He paused. "And because I own it."

My eyes popped. He owned this hotel?

Before I could inquire further, there was a loud knock at the door. Jaime jumped up to open it. A handsome, college-aged waiter wheeled in a white linen-covered cart with two silver dome-covered platters on warmers. I was surprised there was also a chilled bottle of Cristal in a bucket of ice— especially after my embarrassing episode last night.

"Mr. Zander, would you like me to set up a table here or would you prefer to eat in the dining room?" asked the eager-to-please waiter.

"Right here is fine," replied Jaime, pointing to

the area between his chair and the couch.

The waiter magically transformed the cart into a small dining table, complete with linens, utensils, and a votive candle.

"I'll take it from here," said Jaime, slipping the waiter a hundred-dollar bill. The thankful young man scurried out of the suite.

I watched as Jaime expertly uncorked the champagne and poured the bubbly into a pair of flutes.

"Just a little for me," I said hastily as he filled my glass. *Careful, Gloria. Control yourself.* The last thing I wanted was a repeat of last night.

With an amused look, he respected my wishes and filled my flute only halfway. "To a fine meal and fine company." He clinked his glass against mine, brushing his fingers along my flesh. I nervously took a sip of the champagne. The bubbly did little to calm the butterflies swarming my stomach.

His eyes stayed on me as he drank his champagne. "I hope you like filet mignon. I asked for it rare—like you."

The breathy way he said "rare" led me to take another, this time, bigger gulp of my champagne. The truth was, I did like my steaks that way.

He lifted the silver dome. A plate with a small, succulent steak, buttered peas, and potatoes au gratin assaulted my senses. It all looked and smelled divine.

He slid back into his chair and scooted it up to the table. His clean, fresh scent mixed with the mouthwatering aroma of the food.

"Eat!" he ordered.

"What about you?" I asked after placing my napkin on my lap.

"My dish has to simmer. Besides, I want to watch you eat. I'll enjoy it."

Anxiously, I cut into the tender steak and put a forkful of pink meat to my mouth.

His eyes never left me. "Ah, you cut your meat and eat the European way," he mused. "I find that very sexy."

I choked. Madame Paulette had taught me this way of eating. It was one of her many life lessons. "Eating like a European will give you class and mystery," she had told me.

"Swallow!" he ordered.

Nervously, as he watched, I gulped down the first morsel of the meat. Getting it past the big lump in my throat wasn't easy.

I continued to eat my dinner under his intense, watchful gaze. As delicious as the meal was, I was losing my appetite with each bite. In fact, my gut was cramping, and a tingling between my legs was distracting me. Why did he affect me this way?

"Aren't you going to eat?" I asked.

A saucy smile curled on his lips. "I'm getting rather hungry and think my meal might be nicely heated up now." Slowly, he lifted the silver dome covering his entrée.

My eyes practically popped out of their sockets. Artfully displayed on the platter were Rihanna's diamond-studded brassiere and thong.

"Gloria, are you done with your dinner?"

Speechless, I just nodded. I couldn't eat a bite more even if I tried.

"Good. Then stand up."

As if under a hypnotic spell, I did as he asked.

He rose to his feet and came around the dining cart. In one swift, smooth move, he swept down the back zipper of my dress, swooped it over my head, and tossed it to the floor.

Quivering, I stood semi-naked in front of him, clad only in my lacy gray lingerie and silk stockings. And my heels.

His lustful eyes roved up and down my body. I suddenly became very conscious of the scar above my heart that peeked out from my bra, but to my relief, he ignored it.

"I like the way you match your undergarments to what you're wearing."

Madame Paulette had ingrained that in me. In a state of semi-shock, I mumbled a throwaway thanks.

He continued to study me. "You have such a sexy body. Custom-made for your lingerie line. But it's such a shame you don't enjoy what you sell. Let me show you how."

My body, indeed curvaceous, was a trembling mess. Words stayed trapped in my throat while I tried to steady myself on my feet.

"Relax, Gloria. Trust me." He shoved the dining cart out of the way. There was nothing standing between the two of us except a storm of electricity.

He squatted halfway to the floor and clutched my thighs with his warm, manly hands. With his teeth, he snapped opened each garter. I stood motionless as he slid my silk stockings down my long legs. His hands brushed against my skin, sending goose bumps all over me. I anchored my palms on his broad shoulders as he removed my shoes and stockings. The garter and my skimpy lace bikinis were the next to hit the floor. He slipped the shoes back on my feet and then stood up and removed my bra. With my scar in full view, my body didn't move a muscle. A contemplative smile spread across his face as he gazed at me.

"Ah, Gloria, you are so, so, beautiful." He reached for the diamond-studded undergarments and handed them to me. "Please put these on."

What?

"Don' t worry. I had them thoroughly cleaned. They're like brand new."

It wasn't Rihanna's crotch I was worried about. It was mine. I was on fire.

"Put the thong on first. I want to stare at those exquisite tits for as long as I can."

My nerves on edge, I bent over and slipped each high-heeled foot into the leg openings of the thong and then pulled it up until the patch of diamonds covered my patch of gold. The diamonds formed a heart—the iconic signature of Gloria's Secret. All our merchandise bore this insignia somewhere. There was even a heart instead of a dot over the "i" in the Gloria's Secret logo.

He examined me. His eyes seared my flesh.

I felt light-headed. The heat of his gaze mixed with the warmth of the buttery leather. Hot juices gathered between my thighs. He was making me melt.

He smiled. "Perfection. Now, the bra."

With jittery fingers, I slipped on the back-closing bra and fumbled with the clasp. After hooking it, I twisted the bra around, slipped my arms into the straps, and plumped my milky-white globes into the push-up cups. Hearts of diamonds surrounded my erect nipples.

Jaime gazed at me reverently. "You look more beautiful in these works of art than I ever imagined."

My brows rose to my forehead. "You bought them for me?" I asked, finding my voice.

He let out a light, sexy laugh. "No, I bought them *for me* to look at on you."

Semantics. A chill ran down my spine in anticipation of what was next.

"Turn around."

I pivoted on my heels and could feel his eyes on my very exposed ass.

"Beautiful. Now come over here. I think my dinner is ready."

Hesitantly, I stepped into him. In my stilettos, we were eye to eye. Chest to chest. Organ to organ.

His eyes bore into mine. "You're so fucking edible. I bet you're going to taste so good."

Edible...Taste?

In one smooth move, he yanked down the thong to my ankles and dropped to his knees. He gazed up at me with his hungry eyes.

"Spread your legs," he ordered.

They just shifted apart as though I was contractually obliged. In a breath, my buttock cheeks were cupped in his hands, and his mouth was buried in my pussy, sucking and nibbling at my tender flesh.

Why the hell am I letting him do this? What's the matter with me?

"You're so fucking delicious," he moaned. "And so moist."

His hot, velvety tongue swept across the folds of my cleft. "Mmmm. And so sweet." Stroking and licking, he was clearly enjoying his dinner.

I had the answer to my questions. I was enjoying it too. Okay. That was an understatement. I was in a state of rapture. The movements of his aerobic tongue were sending a heat wave through my body. I squeezed my eyes and stifled the moans that were begging to be released. It took all the willpower I had not to squirm. *Control yourself, Gloria!*

And then his tongue stayed in one place—my clit. He alternately flicked it with the tip and rolled circles around it. My body quivered as overwhelming pleasure flooded my brain. I bit down on my lip to quell the sounds clogging my throat.

Still working my nub furiously, he shoved his fingers into my hole. I jolted. There must have been two of them inside, judging by the fullness. He slid them up and down my passage, bringing a new level of erotic pleasure to my being. All the while, his tongue stayed focused on my clit.

Control was no longer an option. I was totally losing it. Whimpers escaped my throat; sweat escaped my pores. Writhing against him in my stilettos, I clung to his shoulders for support as the insufferable throbbing between my legs threatened to undo me. Truthfully, I wasn't sure if I could hold on any longer. He was driving me to the point of no return. *Oh my God. Oh my God. Oh my God.*

"Fall apart for me now, Gloria." As he breathed

my name, I exploded on command with a ragged
scream. Shudders deep inside me competed with
the wet bundle of shuddering nerves between my
legs. I thought I might pass out.

He gripped my hips to steady me and then flicked
my clit one last time, sending yet another orgasm to
my sex. Oh, what this man could do to me!

He finally pulled away and gazed up at me.
With sexy half-moon eyes, he lifted the three, yes
three, deft fingers that had been inside me to his
lush mouth and sucked them. He lowered them and
licked his lips.

"Ah Gloria, you are like fine caviar. I hope you
enjoyed your dinner as much as I enjoyed mine.
Would you like dessert?" he asked before pulling up
the diamond-studded thong and rising to his feet.

I didn't think I could handle dessert, whatever
that was. When I glimpsed the bulge, now bigger,
beneath his sweats, I had an idea. "I'll pass," I said
breathlessly.

"Oh, do you feel sated?" I could tell his eyes were
hungering for more.

"Yes," I stammered. *Very.* "I need to go to sleep."
Shaking, I collected my clothes that were strewn on
the floor.

He smirked at me. "*My* brassiere and thong,
please."

"Right." Before I could get make a move, he
one-handedly unhooked the bra and slipped it
off. Scrunching it in his hand, he pulled down the
diamond-studded thong with the other. I held on to
his broad shoulder for balance as I stepped out of

it. Embarrassment seeped through me. The crotch was now drenched.

He bent over, retrieved his prize and, to my shock, put the soaking wet undergarment to his nose. He inhaled deeply. "I don't think I'm going to wash these."

I donned my dress, not bothering to put my underwear back on. I swept the lacy pieces up in my hands; he didn't need more souvenirs.

"Thanks for dinner." I rushed the words and pivoted toward the door. My body was still throbbing from my head to my toes.

He tugged my braid hard, holding me back. I spun around to face him. "Let go of me."

Gripping my braid, he roped me in closer to him. So close, his breath heated my cheeks. "What are you doing tomorrow?"

"I have a busy day. Store visits. Our Fifth Avenue store is our largest. I'll be there all afternoon."

"Ah, Gloria. All work, no play. I'm going to change that." He did the hair thing again—coiling my braid around his hand. "The hotel has a splendid pool on the top floor. Meet me there at six a.m. when it opens. No one will be there except us. We'll have it all for ourselves...have a little fun and get in some exercise...maybe burn off this meal."

He let me go. As my weak legs carried me to the door, he breathily said, "Don't be late."

"I never am." I didn't turn back to look at him but knew his glimmering eyes were lingering on me, his smile cocky from his little victory.

As I limped down the hallway to my suite, he

called out to me. "Hey, Gloria. Happy Valentine's Day."

A smile that he couldn't see curled on my lips. Confession: It was the best Valentine's Day I'd ever had.

Chapter 8

I THOUGHT FOR SURE THAT I would meet him at the elevator, but he wasn't there. I was wearing the plush white terry cloth robe that came with the room over a Gloria's Secret bright red bandeau bathing suit; it was cut in a way that made my long legs look even longer. I had also packed a bikini but decided on the one-piece because it was more comfortable and enabled me to swim fast without any worry of it falling off. Besides, no bikini could compete with the diamond-studded underwear I'd worn last night. Unable to force that memory away, I pressed the call button and, when the doors slid open, headed up to the pool. I stared down at sparkly flip-flops on my feet—one of our bestsellers last summer—trying impossibly hard not to concentrate on the throbbing that lingered between my thighs.

To my surprise, he was already doing laps up and down the Olympic-size pool when I showed up. His form was beautiful...long, elegant strokes with his brawny arms and long, tapered fingers and powerful kicks that spliced the water with little splashes. Upon catching sight of me on a breath, he finished his lap and lifted himself out of the pool. Dripping wet, his soaked hair slicked back, he broke into that dazzling smile. "Good morning, Gloria. I'm looking forward to our swim together and to seeing you all wet."

My heart skipped a beat. This was the first time I'd seen him without his clothes on—well, almost without his clothes on. He was wearing one of those latex Speedos made for racing that exposed a body that could belong to an Olympic champion. His shoulders were broad; his chest chiseled, his arms sculpted, and his legs long and muscular. For sure, a body of steel. A fine layer of dark hair coated his limbs and, descended from his amazing pecs to the most fabulous V-section I'd ever seen on a man. The package between his toned thighs was sizeable—actually, make that, monstrous—and sent shudders through me. The throbbing between my legs intensified; I could actually hear the thrumming like a heartbeat.

"C'mon, I'll race you for dinner. The winner of two out of three laps gets to pick a restaurant; the loser gets to pay."

"What makes you think I want to have dinner with you, Mr. Zander?"

"Ms. Long, after last night, there's no doubt in my mind."

I bit my lower lip. Tongue-tied, I managed one word: "Fine."

I shrugged off my robe. Jaime's sparkling denim blue eyes ran down my body. "You are simply magnificent. A feast for the eyes. Maybe the winner's prize should be ripping off the other's bathing suit."

I wrinkled my nose at him. "Forget it. A deal is a deal. Come on, let's race."

I was looking forward to the challenge. He had

no idea whom he was dealing with. Having lived in Brighton Beach, I had become a masterful swimmer thanks to the nearby ocean and large community pool. My long lean muscles and broad square shoulders reflected my passion. I still swam regularly in the heated pool at my condo complex. Ha! Little did he know, I was extremely competitive.

We lined up side by side at the edge of the pool's deep end. His slick wet body deliberately brushed against mine, sending a chill up my spine. We wished each other good luck.

"Okay, on your mark, get set, go!" I called out and with that, we both dove into the water.

To my relief, the pool was heated. I wasted no time propelling myself ahead, stroking and kicking furiously. Damn it! Mr. Challenge was keeping up with me, even at the halfway mark. When I got to the other end a mere second before him, I quickly did a flip turn and headed back to where we had begun. On a breath, I stole a glance backward. Ha! My competitor was losing steam and was now several lengths behind me. Picking up speed, I raced ahead and reached the starting point way before he did. Breathing hard, I popped out of the water and, with a smug smile, watched him struggle to meet me. "Fuck!" he cursed under his labored breath.

"I'm thinking of a very expensive restaurant," I taunted and flipped back my heavy wet braid.

"I am, too," he said, catching his breath.

I dwelled on his glistening face. God, he was beautiful, his lush lips moist and his eyes, two glimmering blue pools with crowns of thick lashes. My heart thudded, an unstoppable reaction to the sight of the god-like man beside me and the challenge that faced me. Ha! He was no match for me. One more race and it would be over for sure. This time he said "on your mark," and we took off. I reached the other end way before he did and turned around quickly. I could taste victory. About a third of the way back, I noticed that he was picking up speed. My limbs and lungs burning, I surged ahead. Three breaths later, he passed me; I gaped when I glimpsed his cocky smile. He was beating me to the finish line by several yards. An amused glint flickered in his eyes when I finally reached our starting point. I was panting. He wasn't even breathless. What the fuck? Had he possibly let me win the first race? Faked all that heavy breathing? I was fuming.

"Are you still thinking about a very expensive restaurant?" he asked with playful sarcasm.

I scowled. "Yes!"

He tugged at my thick wet braid. "You're cute when do that little frown thing between your brows."

I was seething. Simply seething. "Cute" was the last thing I was.

The third and final race. The race that would determine who was taking whom to dinner. I mentally psyched myself up for it. *Come on, Gloria, show him!*

"Good luck, Gloria. May the best man win."

"Or woman," I scoffed.

He winked at me as we zoomed off.

I was off to a strong start. *Just focus on the race.* I forced myself not to take any breaths—a means of keeping him out of my field of vision and not letting him distract me. Kicking and stroking at torpedo speed, I flipped around at the other end and finally came up for a much-needed gulp of air. To my horror, there he was...several lengths ahead of me. Calling upon every muscle in my body, I caught up to him only for him to swim ahead of me one more time. He shot me a cocky smile on a breath as he passed me by. Damn him! I couldn't let him win! Furiously, I propelled myself forward, stroking and kicking harder than I'd ever had. We were neck to neck. Breath to breath. Splash to splash. Every muscle in my body stung as I took my last stroke. My head shot out of the water. Clinging to the edge of the pool, I was panting like a dog. I couldn't catch my breath. My waterlogged eyes fluttered. He was in my face. At the finish before me.

"Get over here, you," he rasped. Breathing heavy, he took me in his powerful arms and drew me against him. I was too exhausted to resist. My heart pounded against his; I hadn't been this close to someone else's heartbeat in years. Before I could say a word, he tilted back my head by the tail of my braid and crushed his mouth upon mine. The warmth of his breath heated mine. His kiss was passionate and fierce. I was panting into his mouth. Once again, I was losing control to this outrageous man. I don't know why but I just let him do it. Even deepen the kiss as his tongue parted my lips. Inside my mouth, it did a synchronized swim with mine. Swirling and twirling. It was as if we had practiced these moves for years. He broke away, leaving me breathless for more.

"Wrap your legs and arms around me and just relax."

Without questioning myself, I complied, folding my limbs around his broad shoulders and bum of steel. The buoyancy of the water helped hold me up.

His glistening wet skin brushed against mine. I longed for his mouth. He read my mind. "Ms. Long, you obviously need to be kissed. And kissed often by a man who knows how."

In a heartbeat, he consumed my mouth again, sending carnal waves of desire to my core. I could feel his erection digging into me as I squeezed my legs around him. My hand fisted his slick wet hair. He moaned and I moaned back.

I don't know how long we stayed in this position, when a crotchety voice brought us abruptly to our senses.

"I wish I could do that."

We had company. A slight, elderly, balding man, who was wearing swim trunks two sizes too big for him, was hunched over above us. My face flushed with embarrassment.

"Don't let age stop you," chuckled my companion, not the least bit embarrassed.

"Can you find me one as pretty as her?" cackled the octogenarian and then plowed into the pool with a loud splash-worthy belly flop. He swam away, in quite good form for a man his age.

"Guess I won't be able to fuck you here."

The F-word resounded in my head. Now what was I getting myself into? And why wasn't I running away?

Jaime hauled himself out of the pool and then helped me out. He wrapped me up in my fluffy white robe and then slipped on his. He held me against him, and again I was unable to resist. It felt so good to lay my head on his strong chest against the soft terry cloth.

"Come on, let's take a hot shower together," he said softly in my ear.

"In your suite?" I gasped.

"No, here. There's a great handicapped steam shower in the men's room." He pressed his heavy erection against me. "And right now, I'd say I'm handicapped."

I swallowed hard and let him lead the way, his hand clasping mine. The thought of showering in the men's room made me feel like a very naughty schoolgirl.

There was no one in the men's room. The spacious handicapped shower, complete with support railings and a bench, occupied a corner at the end of a row of shower stalls. We shrugged off our robes and hung them on the hooks bracketing the shower door.

Jaime's hands gripped the top edge of my bathing suit.

"What are you doing?"

"What does it look like? I'm taking off your bathing suit."

"Wait! Remember? This was not part of the prize package!" Too late. The wet suit was already a crumpled heap at my feet.

"Not fair."

"Don't worry." He immediately slid his off too.

For the first time, I got an eyeful of his cock. Holy cow! It was huge. And the veined, pink pillar of flesh was pointed my way. *Run, Gloria!* Forget it! My legs had turned to jelly, and the air had left my lungs.

Taking my clammy hand, Jaime led me into the shower stall. Trailing him, I noticed a series of faint white lines streaking his back. Stretch marks? This was the only imperfection on his otherwise perfect body. They didn't distract from his beauty.

With his free hand, he slammed the glass door shut. He jiggled the shower knob, and a forceful spray shot out from the showerhead. He wrapped his muscled arms around me from behind, spooning my body into his. His powerful arousal brushed against my backside.

The hot water pounded on the two of us. He tightened his grip around me and nuzzled the nape of my neck, then the sides. I'd never realized how sensitive my neck was. The erotic sensation made me tingle all over.

"Gloria, you are so fucking beautiful," he whispered into my ear. He nibbled the lobes then rolled his tongue inside my inner ear. The strangely erotic swooshing sound was turning me on even more.

Slipping off the simple black elastic at the end, he started to undo my braid. Slowly, section by section. I closed my eyes, and when I reopened them, my thick platinum hair hung loose to the base of my spine. He raked his fingers through the long soaked strands.

"I want to see you with your hair down tonight."

Not wanting to think about how long it would take me to blow dry my mane, I asked, "Where do you want to eat with me tonight?"

"I'll eat with you anywhere you breathe."

His words sent a shiver up my spine. A restaurant was not what I was thinking about.

I felt him kiss the top of my head; he buried his nose into my scalp and inhaled.

"Mmmm. I can't get enough of your hair. It's like wet silk." He squirted a dollop of shampoo onto his palm from the canister and then rubbed it gently all over my head. He began to lather the creamy soap into my hair, digging the tips of his deft fingers deep into my scalp. I arched back my head and closed my eyes, allowing myself to savor the sensual physical sensation and erotic squishy sound. God, it felt good. Like a scalp fuck. As he worked conditioner into my hair, I moaned with pleasure. What these beautiful, nimble fingers could do!

Still standing close behind me, he moved his hands to my full breasts and began to knead them, circling and squeezing. His palm passed over the raised scar above my left breast, but he again seemed oblivious to it. In response, I undulated my hips, brushing my backside against his erection. His hips moved with mine.

"They're for real," he murmured, groping my mounds.

I wanted to punch him. "Yes."

"That's what I thought."

Obviously, he'd fondled the surgically enhanced type way too many times. Maybe even Vivien's? I inwardly flinched then relaxed. I had to remember: he was a stud, the gorgeous millionaire kind, who'd probably fucked a gazillion beautiful women. And felt up twice as many breasts. I let it go and let myself enjoy the sensuous massage.

I always knew I had sensitive breasts, but not this sensitive. Each time his thumbs trailed across my nipples, a jolt of pleasure zapped my core. I moaned and moaned again. The peaks grew hard and long, and the more he rubbed them, the more my body throbbed with desire.

Jaime breathed into my ear. "Ah, those perfectly puckered rosebuds of yours are so tender."

Leaving a knowing hand on one tit, he slid the other down my torso until it made its way to the fiery triangle between my thighs. Beelining for my clit, he fingered it with single-minded fury. My own moisture mingled with the shower. My nub hardened beneath his touch as he continued to circle it fast and hard. My breathing grew ragged. He was driving me wild and I wanted, no needed, to come badly.

"Please make me come," I cried out.

He abruptly withdrew his fingers—almost like a punishment for asking. "Not yet, Gloria. I want you do to something for *me* first."

Anything.

He flipped me around and swung my arm up to the liquid soap canister. He squirted a clump onto my palm. "Get down on your knees and wash my cock. I want to see your eyes. So look up at me as you do it."

Without the slightest hesitation, I dropped to my knees and wrapped the hand with soap around the crown of his huge erection. It shot straight out of him and was practically in my face. The heat of it singed my fingertips. My soapy hand skated down the rigid shaft to the base and then glided back up to the tip. How velvety smooth it was! And how big!

Its extraordinary girth fit tightly into the curl of my fingers.

"Good, Gloria. Now squeeze harder and hold my balls with your other hand."

My left hand cupped his heavy sacs as I slid my right hand back down his thick length, applying more pressure. Then back up. I repeated the movements, picking up my pace. My eyes never left his enraptured face. I watched with awe as he arched his head back and parted his luscious lips. A loud groan escaped between them. His balls felt heavier. Was he going to come?

He gazed back down at me with his hooded blue eyes. "Ahh, you're doing it just right. Now, I want you to rinse me off with your mouth."

So, he wanted me to give him a blow job—like I owed him one for last night. Okay. I could handle this. Confession: The thought of giving this beautiful man head excited me. I opened my mouth wide, but before I could take him, he yanked me up by my hair.

"Go down on me standing." He placed his hand on top of my head and pushed it down toward his erection. I had to bend my knees for my mouth to make contact with it.

I flicked my tongue across the bulbous crown, glad to discover that the soap had washed off, and then wrapped my lips around its impressive perimeter. As he let out a moan, I went down on his slick, hard length until I could go no further. My mouth came back up, and I repeated the movements. Again and again. Up and down. Faster and faster. His magnificent cock became my mouth's obsession.

Without breaking contact, I placed one hand on his muscular thigh and the other around the side handicapped railing to give me the support I needed in this semi-squatting position. My thighs were burning. I felt like I was doing one of those loathed "chair positions" with my yoga instructor.

"Oh, baby, you suck me so good. So hard."

I gazed up at him. The expression on his face was one of pure tortured ecstasy. I was amazed how much pleasure I got from pleasuring him. Despite my discomfort, I wanted to please him.

I came up for a quick breath of air.

"Don't. Stop."

Before I could tell him not to worry, he pressed down on the crown of my head, urging me to descend on him once again. This time, my tongue lapped the shaft as I headed back up toward the tip.

He groaned. "I'm going to come in your mouth."

One spurt. Two. Three. He let out a deep guttural grunt and cursed under his breath as his release spilled into my mouth. The taste of it was sweet and salty and surprisingly good. I swallowed every drop.

"We're not done. Suck me dry."

My eyes gazed up at his impassioned face as I feverishly went back down on his cock, taking in only the upper one third into my mouth. Removing my hand from his thigh, I squeezed the base as my mouth bopped up and down. The silky, soaked hair along his groin brushed against the back of my hand.

"Oh, Gloria!" he roared as he coated my tongue one more time. His eyelids lifted. "This time, I want to watch you swallow."

I eagerly gulped it down. Smiling with satisfaction, he withdrew his thick, slick dick. Smiling back, I straightened up, glad not to be in that painful crouching position. My legs felt like Jell-O.

The shower washed away the last traces of his cum. To my shock, his cock was still semi-erect.

"Christ, that was fucking amazing. You never stop surprising me. Now, I'm going to finish what I started."

Smacking a kiss on my lips, he stepped out of the shower. In a split second, he was back. The belt of his terry cloth robe was dangling around his neck. *What the...*

Stopping me in my thoughts, he scooped me up in his arms and then set me down on the teak wood planks of the built-in handicapped shower bench. "Trust me, Ms. Long, *you're* going to be handicapped once I'm done with you."

I eyed the belt. A shudder ran through me. "What are you going to do to me?"

"I'm going to make you fall apart and then attempt to put you back together again."

I snickered. "You think I'm some kind of Humpty Dumpty?"

He smirked. "You're much more fragile. At least on the inside."

My breath hitched. He knew me. "What if someone has to use the shower?"

"They'll knock." He knitted his brows. "Are you on birth control?"

I nodded helplessly. My pills helped me with my cramp-ridden periods.

A smile danced in his eyes. "Good. Now, lie down."

Wait! What about him? He'd probably fucked a gazillion girls. Could I trust him?

"Don't worry. I'm clean. I've been tested. Now, lie down."

Hesitantly, I lowered myself to a reclining position. My torso spread across the length of the bench while my limbs hung over the edge.

"Now, Gloria, I want you to open your mind *and* your legs. For. Me."

In one swift move, he spread my dangling legs and threw my ankles over his broad shoulders. Looming above me, he gazed at my sex. His glorious cock, now almost fully erect again, pointed my way. The shower began to fog up. There was something otherworldly about seeing his god-like body in a cloud of steam.

"You're such a pretty shade of pink. You may, however, be a shade of red when I'm through with you."

I cringed. Was he going to pussy-whip me with the belt?

"Relax. I'm not going to hurt you." *The mind reader.* "But I am going to tie you up. You'll enjoy it. Now lift your arms high."

Relieved, I did as requested. With whip-like speed, he wrapped the long belt around my wrists, binding them together, and then attached them to the handicapped railing directly above me. I writhed my arms to see if I could free myself. Forget it. He had me tied up too tightly.

"I need to get harder, and you need to get horny." He kneeled on the edge of the bench and reached across me to fondle my mountainous breasts.

Crawling on his knees closer to me, he planted his erection into the valley between them and then squeezed the mounds against the shaft. He moaned with pleasure while I, too, got off on the sensuous massage I was getting. Erotic pleasure rushed to my core. Oh God! I was ready! My body was crying out for him while my mind said no. *Gloria, let go. Open your mind!*

"Your breasts are such sweet pillows of flesh," he murmured as he continued to rub them against his cock. "Now let's see, if I've aroused you."

He shoved a finger into my opening. I moaned but wanted something more.

"Ah. You're so hot and wet. But not quite ready."

He pulled his finger out and began to play with my tender clit. Vigorously circling it like a finger-painting child. I groaned.

"How does that feel?"

My clit was a lit up firework ready to explode. I didn't know how much more I could take. I desperately wiggled my bound arms attempting to free myself; it was futile.

"Answer me, Gloria." His tone was demanding.

"Oh, yes!" I moaned.

"Good enough."

Still fingering my clit, he used his other hand to rub the crown of his thick length up and down the folds of my cleft. He was teasing me when I was aching for him to be inside me.

He leaned into me, placing his hands on the bench for support. "I'm going to come inside you now and give you an orgasm that's going to blow that uptight mind of yours to pieces."

"Please," I begged.

He grinned wickedly. "I'm going to fuck you until you can't walk. I'll be carrying you back to your room."

Oh, yes! Handicap me!

Balancing on one hand, he used the other to position his pulsing length. I felt his hot cock at my doorway to pleasure. A thrust away from penetrating me, there was a loud pounding on the fogged-up shower door.

"What's going on in there?"

I recognized the voice immediately. It was the old man who had gone for a swim.

"Fuck!" muttered Jaime. "I'm not going to rush this." He leaped up from the bench and stormed out the shower, leaving me tied up and throbbing. I assumed he was going to return right away with our robes. *Hurry!*

The door re-opened. I gasped. The little old man, shuffled into the shower. His skin was prune-like from his long swim, and a towel was wrapped around his waist. It fell to the wet tiled floor upon seeing me, naked and bound to the handicapped railing. He was not a pretty sight.

"I want whatever he had," he said brightly.

Oh, fuck! He wasn't just an old man. He was a dirty old man! Oh God! Had Jaime abandoned me? Left me helplessly stranded with this horny geezer?

My panic button sounded. Just as my mind skipped to the worst possible scenario, Jaime burst through the shower door. He was wearing his beltless robe and had mine draped over his arm. His large balls and cock, now in a relaxed state, peeked out of the robe opening.

"Excuse me, sir," he said calmly. "My girlfriend needs to take her meds."

Girlfriend? Meds?

He quickly unbound me and helped me put on my robe. I was mortified every which way. Before I could say a word, he swept me up into his arms. The old man looked at us, baffled. "Sorry," said Jaime, as he kick-opened the door and carried me out. "She swoons in showers." Amusement flickered in his eyes.

Once outside the shower, I was simmering mad. "What the fuck? Where the hell did you go? Why did you leave me for so long?" Each question flew out faster than the one before.

A sheepish grin spread across his beautiful face. "Sorry. I had to take a leak. And jerk myself off." He gently set me down on my feet.

I blew out air to release the rage that was consuming me.

"Don't be mad at me. It wasn't my fault. I'll make up for it at dinner."

My lips snarled. "There's not going to be any dinner."

He fisted a clump of my loose tangled hair and tugged at it hard. "Hey, remember what you said. A deal is a deal."

My words. Another life lesson from Madame Paulette. I scoffed at him. "Do you have a place in mind?"

"Raoul's. It's *very* expensive."

I scrunched my face. "Fine. Meet me downstairs at the entrance of the hotel at eight."

"Perfect."

Damn it. I was stuck with dinner. And the possibility that this challenging man who knew how to make me fall apart was going to be in my life in more ways than one.

Chapter 9

I SPENT THE REST OF THE day running around the city doing store checks. We had retail outlets in every borough—except Brooklyn. *Borofskyland.* It irritated Victor that I refused to open a Brooklyn store; it was a missed opportunity, especially since Brooklyn, now a chic place to live, catered to affluent Gen X'ers. The money-hungry opportunist didn't understand it was one place I could never go back to. It held a terrible memory for me and it was too risky. Boris was still living there according to Intelius.com, and I was sure that he'd recognize me immediately.

Thank goodness, I had Nigel to get me around because the city traffic was impossible. As he expertly navigated it, transporting me from one store to the next, I couldn't stop thinking about Jaime Zander. He was unraveling me, bringing me to sensual and emotional places I'd never been before. And I was letting him. I hardly knew this man. It had to stop, especially if we ended up working together. The last thing I needed in either my personal or professional life was a fucked up relationship. I made an executive decision. Over dinner, I was going to bring this all to an end. Just keep everything to business.

The store visits were a welcome distraction.

For the most part, the city retail outlets were all in good order. I enjoyed spending time with the general managers as well as their sales assistants. It was also good to observe first-hand the shopping patterns of customers. I even chatted with several and got some valuable consumer insights. All were very excited about the possibility of Gloria's Secret sex toys.

I caught up with Kevin and Vivien at the Fifth Avenue flagship store in the mid afternoon. We were having a special in-store event there—a fashion show. A scaled-down version of our big extravaganza. There was going to be coverage by one of the local cable channels as well as by numerous bloggers. Gift cards and coupons were being offered to shoppers in attendance. Kevin, as always, was handling everything beautifully. Vivien, however, wore a resentful expression. She had actually e-mailed me that she wanted to go shopping while she was in Manhattan. I had to remind her this was a business trip, not a vacation.

The show went off without a hitch and customers loved it. Sales went through the roof another day in a row. Shortly afterward, Kevin strolled up to me. "Glorious, want to go out for dinner tonight?"

I twitched a regretful smile. "Can't. I'm having dinner with Jaime Zander."

"Oh," chimed in nearby Vivien. "Business or pleasure?" The sarcasm in her voice was hard to miss.

"Strictly business." Though my tone was nonchalant, Vivien eyed me suspiciously.

"Did you know Jaime Zander is one of Manhattan's

most eligible billionaires?" she asked.

I digested this new piece of information. While I'd never seen his name on the Forbes 400 List, I guess if he owned the Walden Hotel and could afford to spend two million dollars on Rihanna's leather undergarments, he must be mega-rich. Though ZAP! was quite a successful ad agency, it didn't seem enough to make Jaime so wealthy. I wondered—how did he make his fortune? Maybe at dinner, I'd find out.

I checked my watch; it was almost six. "I'm going to split. I need to get ready for my dinner."

The thought of having dinner with Jaime Zander made my whole body quiver with anticipation and apprehension. I was anxious about seeing him. Would I be able to keep my emotions—and hormones—in check and keep things purely professional? What concerned me as much was that I was looking forward to seeing him.

The twinkle in Kevin's hazel eyes clued me in that he knew there was something going on between Jaime and me. After all these years together through thick and thin, he could read me like a book. Vivien's eyes, however, were shooting daggers my way.

"Where are you going for dinner?" she asked, her tone snarky.

"Raoul's." I immediately regretted that I told her.

Back at the hotel, I showered and rewashed my hair. I remembered that Jaime had asked me to wear it long and loose. I debated whether to give in to him, but ultimately decided in his favor. It took me almost an hour to blow dry my waist-length locks. There was a reason why I wore it in an easy braid, but I had to admit it looked gorgeous, cascading down my back and over my shoulders like a whimsical cape. My mane of hair was my treasured asset. After my wicked, narcissist mother chopped it off with a meat scissors in a drugged-out fit of rage, I vowed never to cut it short again. My long hair, in some way, was my security blanket. And it covered my scar.

After the blow dry, I did my makeup, keeping it light and simple. I studied my heart-shaped face in the bathroom mirror and was pleased. I looked soft but sexy.

I put on some light jazz and went through my ritual of matching my outfit to my undergarments. The dress I chose was a flowy powder blue chiffon V-neck Valentino that accented my narrow waist and my full breasts without giving too much away. Beneath it, I wore delicate lacy blue lingerie from our popular "Hot Nights" collection—an underwire bra, v-string panty, and matching garter that held up my sheer silk hose. While slithering the stockings up my legs, I'd once again thought about my beloved mentor, Madame Paulette. Sadness swept over me. I was relieved that I had told her my secret. The one that had haunted me my entire adult life. Yet, I still bore the weight of my misdoing on my heart. And the nightmares had never stopped.

Forcing negative thoughts to the back of my head, I stepped into a pair of strappy, silver stilettos that went well with the demure dress. Grabbing a soft blue pashmina shawl and a clutch, I headed toward the elevator. I was purposely fifteen minutes early.

GLORIA'S SECRET   113

I wanted to be at the entrance to the hotel before Mr. Zander. And have the time to rehearse what I was going to say to him about mixing business with pleasure. Okay. Sex. The very thought of his cock sent a rush of wetness to my panties. *Stop it, Gloria. Get a grip! You can't let this man do this to you!*

As I stood anxiously at the hotel's entrance, Vivien came flying in with a bunch of shopping bags in her hand. All of them were from high-end Madison Avenue designer boutiques. A little shocked to see me, she gave me the once-over.

"Enjoy your business dinner," she smirked with an emphasis on the word "business."

I tweaked my lips to smile. "I'll see you down here at 8:30 tomorrow morning. We've got a full day of agency meetings."

Without another word, she skirted past me. Vivien was just too damn impetuous for her own good. Lucky for her, Daddy was Gloria's Secret largest shareholder and Chairman of the Board and protected her surgically enhanced ass. If I could, I would fire the entitled little bitch in a New York minute.

A warm, firm pair of hands on my bare shoulders stopped me in my thoughts. And then through parted hair, I felt soft warm lips nuzzle the nape of my neck. Tingles raced down my spine. I jerked and spun around. Jaime!

I swear my eyes were drooling. Tonight, he was Mr. Preppy—clad in a crisp blue and white striped collarless shirt that was unbuttoned enough to flaunt his taut chest. The shirttail hung loose over tight but not too tight perfectly pressed jeans.

Navy suede loafers covered his sockless feet, and a rich cashmere sweater, almost the same blue as my shawl, wrapped around his broad shoulders. Bottom line...he looked fucking sexy. And smelled intoxicating.

I sucked in a breath. "Your car or mine."

"Mine." He studied me. "My sex goddess, you look like an angel. Blue is definitely your color, and you should always wear your hair that way."

"Thanks," I mumbled, trying to hold it together while he called his driver. Why did he have to say the word "sex"? Though I had mastered my "all good things must come to an end speech," my hormones were already raging. I bit down on my lip.

His car pulled around outside, and as his driver held open the rear passenger door, he slid in after me. I moved away from him. A bemused smile flitted onto his face. "So, Gloria. Are you playing a game tonight? Hard to get?"

I wrinkled my nose. He chuckled. "That nose thing is one of the things I love about you."

I cringed. Why did he say the L-word? He wasn't making it easy for me to stay in control.

He told his driver Orson to take us to Raoul's on Spring Street.

"Have you ever eaten there?" he asked.

I'd heard of the restaurant, one of the city's original French bistros, but had never eaten there. I shook my head.

"The food is delicious. And the atmosphere's great. There's even a fortuneteller who holds court in the loft. Maybe you can ask her about our future."

I cringed. I knew the answer to that already.

There was none.

The restaurant was located not far from Jaime's office. The jam-packed front room resembled a classic Bohemian French bistro, with leather banquet tables and funky paintings, including nudes, hung all over the walls. The attractive brunette hostess, welcomed Jaime with a warm embrace; he was obviously a regular. Flirtatiously looking back at him from time to time, she led us through the crowded, noisy restaurant and then through the busy kitchen to a back room. I couldn't help but wonder if he had fucked her and all the other beautiful women who stopped him along the way.

Unlike the frenetic front room, the back room was low-key and romantic, filled with candlelit tables draped with fine white linens. A glass ceiling added to the atmosphere. We were escorted to a table for two, closest to the blazing fireplace. I could feel the warmth of the fire against my back.

A heavy-set, jovial waiter came to our table. "Good evening, Mr. Zander. What will it be tonight?" As Jaime pondered the menu, the waiter looked me over and smiled. I wondered—was this where Jaime brought all his fucks? And how many had sat in this chair before me? I mentally kicked myself. Why should I care? This wasn't even a date; it was a business dinner. And I was about to set the womanizer straight.

Jaime gazed up at me. The flickering candlelight and blaze in the hearth bathed his face in a soft glow, making him even more breathtakingly gorgeous than he already was. Despite myself, tingling desire was spiraling inside me. Damn it! *Stay in control, Gloria*, I silently chided.

"Gloria, I hope you don't mind if I order for the two of us. The steak tartare is divine and so is the artichoke. And we'll share a bottle of Bordeaux. We'll have the Latour 2009 Controllé right away," he told the waiter. The waiter smiled and sauntered off with our order.

The wine came quickly. The waiter poured a little into Jaime's glass. Jaime sampled it and then nodded with approval. The waiter continued to pour wine for both of us. After he parted, Jaime clinked his goblet against mine.

"To winning," he said with a seductive smile.

I twitched a smile back at him, wondering if he was referring to our swimming competition, the Gloria's Secret account, or me. Or all of the above.

After a few sips, Jaime eased into conversation. His voice was deep and sultry, and his long-lashed eyes held me captive.

"So, Gloria, tell me something about yourself that I haven't already read online."

"What exactly do you know about me?" I countered.

"Not much...Self-made business woman extraordinaire. Built Gloria's Secret into a billion-dollar company from the ground up."

This was true. After Kevin and I touched down in LA, we stayed at a rundown Hollywood motel until we found a charming two-bedroom apartment to share in Beachwood Canyon. We were able to secure it with a first and last month deposit from the money we had stolen from Boris. Kevin quickly found work as the manager of a hot Hollywood night club, frequented by celebrities, and I, once recovered from my gunshot wound, used the money to rent some studio space downtown and to purchase bolts of lace and silk as well as a dozen used sewing machines and necessary supplies. Once settled in, I hired a handful of talented, eager to work laborers to stitch up my lingerie designs. I shortly found a small, affordable storefront on Hollywood Boulevard to sell my wares. Gorgeous French-inspired lingerie at a reasonable price.

With the help of Kevin, who sent the "beautiful people" who frequented his club to my no-name boutique, my business boomed. Women and men alike fell in love with the innovative, sexy, and reasonably priced undergarments; it became the word-of-mouth, in-the-know place to shop for lingerie...leading me to call my boutique, Gloria's Secret. With my success, I was able to secure a small business loan and six months later, I opened the flagship store, Gloria's Secret, in the Beverly Center, a popular LA mall. The store was an overnight success; a catalogue followed along with a robust website. Kevin quit his job to become my partner and head of Public Relations and Marketing. One year later, enter billionaire businessman Victor Holden, who smelled a winner, invested millions, and took the company public. The rest is history. One store grew to thousands worldwide and a billion dollar a year business.

I took another sip of my wine. Meeting Jaime's gaze, I didn't go into details. "What you see is what you get."

"So far, I like what I've seen." He paused. "And I like what I've gotten."

The double entendres weren't lost on me. I shifted in my seat and crossed my legs under the table to quell the twitching sensation between them.

"But what's that scar on your chest?"

My breath caught in my throat. I almost spit up the wine. He *had* noticed the scar. The reminder of everything I wanted to forget.

"None of your business," I snapped at him.

"Ah, so Gloria has a secret."

Damn him! He was unnerving me. There was no way I was going to open up to this man about my past. That one regrettable moment in time. I didn't want to go there. It was bad enough to live it every waking hour and in my dreams. I quickly changed the subject, focusing on him.

"So, Mr. Zander, tell me, how did you get into advertising?"

"I had a talent. An artistic one. Rather than going to college, I came East and set up meetings with one ad agency after another to show them my portfolio."

I was intrigued. "And then what happened?"

"I got hired by one of the major Madison Avenue agencies—which I'm sure you've met with—to be an art director. While I was touted as a wunderkind, the corporate world was not for me. Too many rules; too much bullshit. I stuck it out for five years, then finally called it quits. A few key clients left with me. Long story short...they rounded up some investor money, and I started ZAP! *Z*ander *A*nd *P*eople."

He was self-made like me. I was awed, but didn't

show it. "So, how did you become a billionaire?"

"Ah, so you fooled me. You've done your research too. I'm impressed."

I wasn't about to tell him that Vivien leaked this tidbit to me though it was fairly obvious.

He sipped his wine. "I inherited several million dollars from my mother, and during the recession a few years ago, I made some lucky investments."

"So you were born with a silver spoon in your mouth."

"Hardly." Jaime's tone darkened. "My mother married someone very wealthy when I was thirteen."

"It must have been fun being a rich kid."

"Money comes with benefits. It also comes with baggage."

"Oh, is that your tagline for your poor little rich boy poster?"

Jaime's eyes flared making me immediately regret what I'd just said. His somber expression suggested that his childhood memories, like mine, might not be happy ones. Perhaps, he was harboring some dark secret too. I flashed back to the faint white marks on his back. Scars? Before I could say a word, the steak tartare and artichoke arrived. Jaime's face brightened. The attentive waiter refilled our wine goblets and then scurried off.

I imbibed more wine. The smooth, rich liquid poured down my throat and coursed through my bloodstream. I was loosening up. *Slow down, Gloria. You don't want to get drunk.*

Jaime cut off the voice of my inner conscious. "Spread your lips, " I heard him say.

I found myself spreading my legs.

Jaime let out a sexy little laugh. "I was referring to your mouth. I want to give you your first taste of the steak tartare."

I felt flushed with embarrassment. He was affecting me again. The area between my inner thighs was getting hot and wet. This was not supposed to be happening. I was losing control!

"Excuse me, I have to use the restroom," I said, leaping to my feet. I needed to get away from him. Compose myself. Focus on business.

"It's in the front of the restaurant, up the stairs," he said, eyeing my body. "I'll be here waiting for you."

I felt his eyes on me the entire time as I made my way to the packed front room and up a rickety spiral staircase. There was a long waiting line to the ladies' room.

A portly, dark-haired woman who resembled a gypsy was stationed at a table outside it. "Let me tell you your fortune, my dear," she called out to me.

Usually, I never did these kinds of things, thinking they were shams, but tonight my unease tempted me, and I really didn't want to wait in line.

I lowered myself into the worn velvet chair facing her.

"You are very beautiful."

"Thank you," I said as she studied my face.

"Your eyes, one brown, one blue, tell me a lot about you. You are two very different people who share the same face. A woman of contradictions. One side of you is light and seductive, the other dark and secretive."

I inwardly gasped. How did she know?

"Let me see your palm." She grasped my right hand and flipped it so that my palm was in full view.

Her eyes grew wide.

"What is it?" My voice was shaky.

"You are losing control of your life. There is a man."

Christ! Jaime Zander was written all over my hand.

She shook her head and bit down on her lip. Her gaze slowly met mine. "I usually tell people good things they want to hear, but I must tell you the truth."

My heart hammered.

"You are in grave danger. Someone is out to get you."

I shuddered. Boris Borofosky! I'd heard enough. I jumped up from the chair and hurried to the restroom. Thankfully, it was now free.

With my dress raised to my thighs and my panties and garter lowered to my knees, I sat on the toilet longer than I needed. I was shaking. Was Boris on my trail? Was he seeking revenge? Was my life in danger? Wait! That wasn't possible. I knew from Madame Paulette that he didn't even know my name. So, he couldn't possibly know where I lived or what I did. Or where I was this very minute. I took a deep calming breath. Besides, that woman was probably a charlatan though she did seem to know the effect Jaime Zander was having on me. Yes, he was making me lose control, but by hell or high water, I was going to put an end to that tonight. Yet, at the very thought of him, the pulsing between my thighs intensified, and I could feel myself heating. I dragged my hand over my cleft. The folds were even hotter and wetter than I imagined. My fingertips could actually feel the throbbing. For a minute, I thought about masturbating, to put myself out of my glorious misery. Instead, I peed and washed up. My hormones were back to raging. Damn that man!

Jaime's eyes contemplated me as I headed back to the table.

"Are you okay?" he asked as he rose to his feet and pulled out my chair.

"Yes." In truth, I was all hot and bothered.

"Good." Returning to his seat, he refilled our wine glasses. There was a roguish glint in his eyes.

"So let's pick up where we left off." He scooped up a forkful of the steak tartare. "Now, part your lips, Gloria."

Again, the sexy command. This time I did as he asked. My lips spread apart.

"I love fine raw meat," he purred as he shoveled a taste of the rare delicacy into my mouth. The velvety, moist meat laced with a hint of Worcestershire sauce was beyond delicious. It totally obliterated any trace of Boris in my head. I immediately wanted more. The gorgeous mind reader fed me another heaping forkful. I swallowed. Tingles rose from my core.

He helped himself to a taste. He savored it before swallowing. "Did you know that steak tartare is an aphrodisiac?"

"I read that somewhere." Being in the sexy lingerie business, I was actually quite knowledgeable about what turned women on. And right now, I was fucking turned on. I wanted this gorgeous man to ravage me.

I jolted. Under the table, I felt something slide under my dress and snake up my thigh-high silk stocking past my garters to my middle. Holy Fuck! It was his bare foot, and it was running circles over my mound.

"Ah, Gloria, your pussy feels so hot and wet beneath those lace panties of yours." He paused. "They are powder blue, right?" he asked with a roguish grin.

"Yes," I gasped. His foot was now rubbing hard against my clit. I was getting more feverish by the second as he pushed me toward the edge. My fingers clutched the corners of the white-linen covered table.

"I think you should stop," I said between clenched teeth.

"There's a difference between I think and I want. Do you *want* me to stop?"

"Yes," I said breathily.

"Your mouth says 'yes,' but your pussy screams 'no.'"

Oh, God! This man got me. He continued massaging, adding vertical strokes up and down my soaking wet cleft. The pleasure and pressure were so intense I thought I would yelp. I dug my fingernails into the table and chewed my lip, trying hard not to scream. Jesus, how would I look if I broke loose?

Jaime shot me a cocky, confident smile. I wanted to rip it off his face with my teeth.

"Gloria, you want to lose control. Do it!" he commanded as he jabbed his big toe into my pussy.

I exploded. Ripples of ecstasy swept through me.

It took all my willpower not to scream out. "Oh, God!" I moaned under my breath.

His satisfied eyes bore into me. "Now, it's time to move onto the steamy artichoke, another natural aphrodisiac."

Barely recovered from my mind-blowing orgasm, I eyed the thistle-leafed delicacy sitting in the middle of the table and jolted again. Beneath the table, a hand clutched my calf. Fuck! My turn to play footsy? My already rapid heartbeat accelerated as he maneuvered off my silver sandal and placed my foot on the mound between his legs. His steamy delicacy. The warmth of his swell beneath my sole intensified the throbbing between my inner thighs.

He began rubbing my foot up and down his arousal. I could feel it harden and expand beneath my arch. He hissed. There was nothing I could do with him holding my foot prisoner but wait anxiously for him to come.

And then the movements below ceased. My foot rested on his erection. The sole of my foot was burning.

His glimmering eyes burned a hole in mine. "I'm not going to force you make me come. That would be too much for me here. Too embarrassing. I just want to remind you what you do to me, my beautiful angel."

Oh my God. He called me "angel." His beautiful angel. My heart was melting like the candle on the table. How could one man, one word, do this to me?

Still holding my foot on his length, he peeled off an outer leaf of the large artichoke with his spare hand and dipped the tender edge into the side of melted butter. He raised the leaf, dripping with butter, to my lips. My breath hitched.

"Suck!" he ordered.

I clenched my teeth around the soft buttery artichoke meat and sucked it off the leaf. He discarded the remains onto his plate. With his index finger, he gently wiped off the little bit of butter that had fallen onto my lower lip. He inserted his butter-coated finger into his mouth and moaned.

"Now, you feed me a buttery leaf."

I peeled off a large outer leaf and repeated his action.

"Mmmm. Perfection," purred Jaime, rolling his tongue over his lush upper lip.

We continued this back and forth consumption of the artichoke until we were down to the heart.

"The heart is the very best part," he proclaimed, his eyes now hooded.

I simply nodded, my foot still resting upon his hard, hot cock. I was in a trance. My head was spinning, and my blood was looping through my body like a rollercoaster. *Hold on, Gloria!*

"Did you know that a woman's heart is her real G-spot? You hit that and everything comes apart."

Trembling, I watched as he stabbed his fork into the fuzzy artichoke center.

"Gloria, I want to win your account. Your cunt. And your heart."

My breath caught in my throat. I couldn't say a word even if I knew what to say.

"And I'm going to win each. One by one, starting with your account."

I impulsively withdrew my foot from his erection.

Business. It was time to talk business. That's what this dinner was all about. I reinforced myself with a deep breath.

"Mr. Zander, if you are planning on doing business with me—that is, if you indeed have the good fortune of winning the Gloria's Secret account—then I suggest we keep our relationship purely professional."

He burst into laughter, totally unnerving me once again.

"Come on, Gloria. Can you can seriously sit here and say you don't want me?"

I was speechless. Flushed and speechless.

"Doesn't the thought of your pussy submitting to me anywhere make you wet with want?"

Steeling myself, I said, "Go to hell, you arrogant egotistical asshole."

He laughed even harder and then looked straight into my eyes.

"Gloria, I've wanted you from the moment I set on eyes on you."

Our first elevator encounter flashed into my head. Face-to-face. Breath to breath. His organ a fist away from mine.

"Even before the elevator. The moment I saw your photo online, I wanted you."

Wait! Was I hearing that right? He was playing me on the elevator? He'd always wanted me? I was in a bit of a fog from all the wine. And stimulation. Was I dealing with some kind of Christian Grey except fifty shades sexier? At least, in my eyes.

"I don't think I'm your type," I stammered.

He snorted. "You're right. I usually prefer

brunettes and like my women to be petite and totally submissive. But that's why you intrigue me, Ms. Long. I never have to pursue woman; they pursue me. You're a challenge. On the outside, you wear armor; underneath you wear lace. Your outerwear says don't touch; your underwear says touch me everywhere. You may be a powerful woman, but the challenge is to unleash the power inside you."

Holy shit! He barely knew me, yet he knew me inside and out. As I sat there wordless and numb, he leaned across the table and ran his fingertips through my long, flowing tresses.

"And by the way, thank you for wearing your hair loose."

I forced a small smile.

"You wouldn't have worn it that way if you didn't want to please me."

Every fiber of my being twitched. He was right!

A crazy-wicked grin spread across his face. "Come here, you." Rising from his chair, he leaned across the table, fisted a handful of my loose platinum locks, and pulled me toward him. His lips were coming my way. As they brushed against mine, I closed my eyes.

"Well, hello, Gloria."

An all-too-familiar aloof voice startled me. My eyes snapped open, and I jerked away from Jaime. Fuck! It was Victor, dressed in a gray pinstriped three-piece suit, with his daughter, Vivien, draped on his arm. Sandwiched in a tight fuchsia mini dress, that revealed everything, and matching stilettos, she could have easily been mistaken as his high-priced hooker.

Jaime's face darkened. Silent daggers went back and forth between the two men. Was Victor still simmering because Jaime had outbid him on the Rihanna undergarments?

Vivien's pillowy lips parted. "Hi, Jaime." Her voice was a deep sexy rasp. "Fancy meeting you here."

Fancy meeting you here? Give me a fucking break. She knew exactly where we were having dinner. I studied her. She was petite and brunette. Jaime's "type." Reflecting on her behavior at the Gloria's Secret Fashion Show and after-party, I wondered— had she and Jaime had sex? Was she one of Jaime's submissives? There was something more than met the eye going on here. I sucked in a breath.

Jaime responded. His voice was as cold as dry ice. "Nice to see you."

Victor's turn. "So, Zander, I understand from my daughter, you're courting the Gloria's Secret account." A smug smile slithered across Vivien's face.

Before Jaime could respond, I hastily chimed in, "Actually, Victor, it's the other way around. I'm courting him. I'm impressed by his creativity."

Victor was stunned into silence.

Jaime shot me a surprised look and then broke into a sexy, grateful smile.

"Why, thank you, Ms. Long. I hope tomorrow we can seal the deal." He came around the table and pulled back my chair, signaling me to stand up too. As I got to my feet, Victor's steely eyes ran down my body. I could feel him mentally undressing me. "Gloria, you exhibit poor judgment when it comes to men."

I scowled. "That's not for you to judge."

Jaime's eyes narrowed and his lips pressed thin. He clenched his hands so tightly his knuckles turned white. One fist rose. My heart raced. Was he going to punch Victor?

To my relief, he relaxed his hand. "Come, Gloria. We should talk business," he gritted.

Vivien sneered while her father remained steely faced. As Jaime ushered me to the entrance of the restaurant, I could feel Victor's eyes on me the whole time.

"Wasn't I supposed to pay for dinner?" I asked while he called his driver Orson on his cell.

"No need. As of yesterday, I own the restaurant."

The drive back to the hotel was fraught with uncomfortable, tense silence. Brooding, Jaime kept his distance. Maybe, he heeded my words. That is was best to keep our relationship purely professional. Still buzzed from the wine, mixed emotions and questions swirled around in my head. So much had gone down tonight. I was dealing with a potential Christian Grey in my life who definitely had some fucked up issues of his own. And I had my own share of fuckedupness that I was not sharing with him. Finally, as we neared the hotel, I broke the thick silence, deciding to get some answers to questions that could effect our potential business relationship.

"What the hell is going between you and Victor? You know, he's the Chairman of Gloria's Secret and wields a lot of power."

"He's nothing to me," Jaime hissed.

I didn't believe him, but the tone of his voice set up a don't-go-there wall.

"What about Vivien?"

"What about her?" he snapped back.

"Have you ever fucked her? She seems your type."

He took a long second to answer. "No."

Again, I didn't believe him, but let it be. "You know, if you do win the Gloria's Secret account, she may be your point person. She's my assistant, and she's being groomed, under her father's orders, to take over marketing."

"I'll deal with it," he said curtly.

The elevator ride up to our floor was no less tense. He accompanied me down the long corridor to our rooms. When I reached mine, I broke away from him and ransacked my bag for my card key. Damn it. I couldn't find it. I must have left it in my other purse.

"Looking for this?" Jaime was in my face, holding up a card key. His mood had lightened.

"That's my card key?" *He had easy entry to my suite?*

He grinned sheepishly. "I had it made the night you were passed out drunk."

He flipped me around and pressed me against the door, pinning me against it with his hips. I could feel the heat of his arousal against my belly through my thin chiffon dress. My breath hitched in my throat as he grabbed my arms and raised them over my head. Like shackles, his fingers locked around my wrists, holding my fisted hands tight against the slab of wood. Once again, I was his prisoner. His to control. Moving in close to me, his hooded eyes bore into mine.

"Let's finish what we started, Gloria, before that prick interfered."

My eyes stayed wide open as he crushed his warm lips onto mine. Every part of my body tingled, from my head to my toes. As the kissed deepened with the entry of his tongue, my core ached. Wanting so much more than his tongue inside me. Desperate moans escaped my lips.

He slid the card key into my door and kept me pinned against it as he pushed it open, his mouth never leaving mine. Finally, he withdrew from my mouth. My breathing was shallow, his harsh and heated.

"Gloria..."

Oh, the breathy way he said my name!

"...I meant what I said. I want to own all of you. Every breath, every heartbeat, every surface of your body, and every bit of what's inside you."

His words sucked the air out of my lungs. I couldn't breathe. Couldn't speak. Couldn't swallow. He was having that effect on me all over again.

"Do you want to come in?" I finally managed, aware of the possible double entendre of my words as an afterthought. My core was silently crying out for him.

Still pinning my arms above my head to the door with one strong hand, he raked the fingers of the other through my tumbled hair. He smirked. "No. I want you to lust for me during my pitch tomorrow."

His eyes burned a hole into mine, setting me afire with desire. He curled a clump of my hair around his long fingers.

"Oh, angel, you have no idea how much my cock wants to be inside that soaking wet pussy of yours, but from here on in, we're going to take it one step at time. First your account...then your cunt."

He smacked a kiss onto my lips. "Good night, Ms. Long. I want to prepare for my first pitch. The second one will be a piece of cake."

With that and a diabolical wink, he left me plastered on the door, my knees so weak I thought I would sag down it. Fuck him! He was now controlling me with torture.

I masturbated my way to sleep, wishing that I had one of those new Gloria's Secret sex toys to expedite my climax. As I came, Jaime Zander's beautiful face filled my head. Drifting off, I looked forward to his pitch and wondered if he would ever win my heart—something no man had ever done except my beloved Kevin. One thing was for sure... he was already under my skin.

Chapter 10

MY WAKE-UP CALL SOUNDED AT the crack of dawn. Two minutes later, there was a knock at the door—my wake-up coffee, something I couldn't live without. Groggily, I threw off the delicious duvet and staggered to the door. After the waiter set the coffee and cream down on a small table, I signed the check and handed him a generous cash tip.

Sipping the steamy rich brew, I checked my schedule on my iPhone calendar. It was a crazy busy day. All day long, I had meetings with one advertising agency after another to hear their pitches. The ZAP! pitch was the last one at five p.m. At the end of the day, my team and I would decide on which agency was going to get the Gloria's Secret account. And then I would be on the corporate jet heading back to Los Angeles.

While the caffeine set my brain in action, I couldn't stop thinking of Jaime Zander. I was as excited as I was anxious about seeing him again. Part of me wished that the ZAP! meeting was the first one—just to get it over with. I had no idea how I was going to get through the other meetings without being distracted by the anticipation of seeing him. I wasn't use to a powerful man rendering me powerless.

I showered and got ready. There was only one

solution to the Jaime problem. I needed to look and feel extra powerful today. In control. Fierce. I added a thick layer of mascara to my long eyelashes and hint of blue eye shadow to bring out the intimidating color of my one blue vs. brown eye. I whipped my long hair into a tight French braid. Lastly, instead of the Gloria's Secret lip-gloss I usually wore, I applied a brilliant shade of red lipstick to my full lips. "Red lips can rule *zee* world," preached my mentor, Madame Paulette.

The outfit I chose was all about power and control—a winter white fitted Chanel suit—perfect for an Ice Queen—and a pair of killer Louboutin black patent stilettos that made me over six feet tall. Beneath my suit, I boosted my confidence with an ivory lace push-up bra from our Sexy Angels collection that matched my bikinis and garter. The sheer black silk stockings I selected made a dramatic contrast with the suit and went well with my jet bead necklace and earrings. Grabbing my purse and briefcase, I headed out the door. I was powered up, ready to take on the various pitches and Jaime Zander.

The elevator once again took its time coming. So much for the saying, "clothes make the person." My short-lived self-confidence morphed into anxiety. I feared the elevator might be broken, never get here… and that at any moment, Jaime might show up. My eyes darted back and forth between the elevator and his room down the hallway. I sighed with relief when the elevator arrived first. I scuttled into it, and blew out another breath of air when the elevator doors closed sans Mr. Zander.

Kevin, dressed in skinny black leather jeans and a tight knit pullover, was waiting for me in the lobby. He gave me a hug. "Morning Glory, you look sensational!"

"Thanks. Where's Vivien?"

Kevin rolled his eyes. "Late as usual."

Damn her! She had no respect for anyone's time except her own. Ten minutes later, she showed up acting like the queen had arrived. Carrying an unnecessary fur coat over her arm, she was dressed in a tight, low-cut purple mini dress and thigh-high black leather boots with mile-high heels. Her outfit was totally inappropriate for our round of meetings. It screamed: Fuck me! Because she was so late, I couldn't ask her to change into something more businesslike. The truth, knowing the vixen's taste in clothes, she likely had nothing more conservative to change into.

She shot me an obsequious smile. "So, how was your dinner with Jaime Zander?"

None of your fucking business. "Very productive." I kept my voice very businesslike. "I'm looking forward to his pitch."

"So am I," chirped Vivien with a smirk. "I'm sure he'll enjoy seeing me again."

Inside, I sizzled. There was definitely something going on between the two of them.

Each meeting was more disappointing than the one before. While the agency heads and their teams pitched us with enthusiasm, everything was SOS. Same Old Shit! A gorgeous big-boobed beauty posing in scanty lingerie. It didn't matter if she was sprawled on a bed or squatting wide-legged on chair. I was looking for something more. Something beyond the obvious that Gloria's Secret equaled sexiness. I was looking for a story. A story of seduction.

My stomach bunched up with nerves as Nigel drove us downtown to our last meeting with ZAP! While I'd managed to keep Jaime Zander on the back burner for most of the day, I now faced the reality of seeing him again. I reapplied a coat of red lipstick. I needed to stay in control, not let him get to me.

We got there a little before five. Jaime's gorgeous assistant Ray promptly greeted us in the reception area and offered us waters. I immediately caught sight of the sparks flying back and forth between Ray and Kevin. Ha! I knew Ray was his type! I shot a knowing glance over to Kev. He mouthed the word "hot." Vivien rolled her eyes. A beaming Ray led us back to the conference room. Already seated at the large conference room table was a geeky twenty-something girl next to whom Ray took a seat. I took in my surroundings. Like the rest of the office, the windowless conference room was warm and creative. There was a large flat screen TV on one of the walls and posters of successful ZAP! ad campaigns on the others. Facing me was a large canvas-covered easel. I wondered—was this the pitch?

"Jaime will be here shortly," announced Ray. My heartbeat sped up at the mention of his name.

On cue, Jaime came flying into the room. I inwardly gasped. He was dressed in a tapered, perfectly tailored black suit, crisp white dress shirt, and a stunning black and blue patterned tie that accentuated his broad shoulders and brought out the blue in his eyes. I'd never seen him in suit before. Holy shit! Today, of all days, he was sexy Mr. Powerful. He took a seat at the head of the table next to me.

His eyes instantly connected with mine, and I could already feel the electricity in the air. I nervously played with my strands of beads.

"Hi, Jaime," purred Vivien. "Great suit."

"Thank you," he replied stiffly.

My blood curdled. What was with them? I was growing more and more convinced that they had some kind of thing going on.

Jaime turned his attention to me and asked me to introduce everyone. He, in turn, introduced Ray, his assistant and protégé, and the funky young woman, Chloe, who was his head copywriter.

"So, Ms. Long, should we get straight into the pitch?"

"That would be good." My tone was very businesslike despite the fact that I was buzzing all over. Damn him! The smartass knew his suit would affect me.

He flashed a smug smile that was intended only for me. "Excellent." He rose to his feet and strode over to the easel. My eyes followed him.

"Ladies and gentlemen..." He swept off the canvas. "Gloria's Secret. Let yourself be carried away."

I gasped out loud. Facing me on a board, in fifty shades of gray, was the black-and-white image of a beautiful blindfolded woman with long platinum hair, who was being carried down a sweeping staircase

by a breathtaking, bare-chested Adonis. Lying limp
in his brawny arms, she wore leather and lace—a
skimpy bra, bikini bottom, and garter that held up
sheer black stockings on her long dangling legs. Her
ankles were bound together by satin shackles as
were her wrists. I totally got it. She was submitting
to her sex god. Letting him take her. To his bed.
Or perhaps to his dungeon! Oh my God! This was
exactly the story I was looking for. This was the new
Gloria's Secret advertising campaign—all in one
line. *Gloria's Secret. Let yourself be carried away.*
I could immediately imagine in my head the print
ad and television commercial. And the zillion hits
on You Tube and our website. I loved the idea of
shooting the campaign in black-and-white sepia
tones. Fifty shades of gray! So fucking fresh! So
fucking forward! So fucking sexy! It gave me the
fucking chills.

Breathless, I asked Vivien what she thought.

She scowled. "I like it, but I think the woman
should be a brunette. Our research shows that men
prefer women with dark hair."

True, but our research also showed that most
women fantasized about being a blonde. I turned
to my second-in-command. My dear, lifelong friend
who made everything happen.

"Kev, what do you think?"

"I think it's fan-fucking-tastic!"

That's exactly what I thought. *Fan-fucking-tastic!*
I could count on Kevin for his brutal honestly and
to tell like it is. I so loved him!

Jaime's lush lips curled into a smug smile. He
was a fucking genius and he knew it.

"Do you have any questions?" he asked.

Only one jumped to mind. "Mr. Zander, whom do you see doing the voice-over— a man or woman?"

His lustful eyes lingered on me. "Definitely a male voice. It's a story of seduction."

My breath hitched before smiling my approval. "Mr. Zander, please have your business affairs people call mine. I'd like to put this campaign on the fast track."

"Excellent," said Jaime, his velvety voice still very businesslike. He thanked his team and dismissed them. The last bit of eye contact between Ray and Kevin did not go unnoticed.

He gazed at me. "Before you leave, Ms. Long, I'd like to have a word with you alone."

I signaled with a jerk of my chin for my team to leave.

Vivien pitched a snit fit. "Excuse me, but don't you think I should stay? I mean, this would be such a good learning experience for me. I could even be the point person on this campaign."

"Vivien, please just go." My voice was authoritative. "I'll catch you up back at the hotel."

"Fine." She stabbed the word at me. With an arrogant fling of her hair, she reluctantly stood up and followed Kevin out of the conference room. Her hips swayed with sexy defiance. At the doorway, she turned her head and shot Jaime an arresting smile. "I'm looking forward to working with you," she purred and then disappeared.

Her words got under my skin. I didn't trust her. Not one bit.

Jaime pushed a button on a wall panel, and the

conference room door slammed shut. Nervous edgy anticipation swept over me. My eyes stayed fixed on his tall lean frame as he loped around the table in my direction. Stopping behind me, he played with my braid, feathering the ends of it against the nape of my neck. The ticklish sensation sent goose bumps crawling all over me.

"So, Gloria, I've won your account."

"Yes. Congratulations."

He let go of my braid and began to knead my shoulders. His touch sent a tingle down my spine.

"Now, I want to win your cunt."

My shoulders heaved and my body tensed. "I think you should stop."

"Come on, Gloria. After yesterday, you know you want me as much as I want you."

Damn it! It was true. A carnal wave of desire rolled through me.

He kneaded deeper. "Relax, angel. You need to let go. Trust me. Trust my every decision and move. Especially if we're going to be working together."

I chewed my lip and nodded.

"Good."

He released my shoulders. Before I could blink, something whipped around my eyes.

"What are you doing?" I shrieked.

"What does it look like? I'm blindfolding you." I felt him tie a strip of fabric tightly behind my head. A band of darkness shrouded my eyes.

I nervously touched my fingertips to the blindfold. The textured fabric was silky —for sure his tie.

"Why are you doing this?"

"I'm teaching you to trust me. Can I trust you

not to take it off?"

Speechless, I nodded.

He lightly kissed the back of my neck. "You just got your first 'A.' Are you feeling more relaxed?"

"Yes," I gasped. Trust *me*, relaxed was the last word I'd use to describe how I felt. Every nerve ending in my body was buzzing with anticipation.

"Stand up. I'm going to undress you."

"What if someone comes in?" I stammered.

"Don't worry, the door's locked. Now please stand up."

I rose to my feet, my legs unsteady. The first thing to go was my suit jacket. So much for power dressing. He was rendering me powerless.

"Ah! Chanel! Size 6. With those tits of yours, I had you pegged for an 8. Very impressive."

I didn't flinch or say a word as he tore off my blouse and yanked down my skirt. In a few short heated breaths, I was stripped down to my ivory lace lingerie and my jet black beads. And the lace-trimmed silk stockings and Louboutin heels. A chill swept over me.

"Ah, Gloria. So apropos, you would wear white lace to celebrate our union. Like a bride." He nuzzled the sensitive area between my shoulder blade and neck and played with my bra strap, his fingers grazing my scar. My pounding heart struggled to stay calm.

"You know, the type of lingerie a woman wears provides an outer expression of her inner sexuality."

Madame Paulette had once told me more or less the same thing.

He continued. "And I'd say, Ms. Long, judging by

the underwear you have on, you're bottling up a lot of sexual energy. I'm going to unleash that."

Bottling? I was overflowing with lust. I could actually hear bottle caps popping as he bit open the back clasp of my bra, his teeth grazing my sensitive flesh. He slid it off me and let it fall to my feet. Exposed, my breasts quivered. With a concomitant moan, his soft hands cupped my full mounds and warmed them. He squeezed them together and massaged them. Heat and moisture rushed to my core as my nipples peeked beneath his palms.

He breathed into my ear. "It'll be hard to find someone as beautiful and sensuous as you to cast in the new Gloria's Secret campaign."

"I thought you loved a challenge," I said, squeezing out the words.

"I do," he said, flutter kissing every part of me.

He flipped me around and lifted me onto the conference room table. I could feel the hardness of the wood beneath my buttocks.

"Lie down, Gloria."

I did as told, stretching myself across the length of the table. My chest rose and fell, my breasts still quivering.

I felt him tug at my red-soled stilettos. "Do you know what these shoes are?"

"They're Louboutins," I stammered. *And they cost a fucking fortune.*

"They're Louboutins to you. But I call them 'fuck me' shoes. That's why women wear them."

He was right. The scantily clad models in our Gloria's Secret catalogue only wore the highest of high heels. I shivered as he slipped them off, one by one, and heard them tumble to the floor.

He clasped my feet in his large, warm hands. His thumbs dug into my silk sheathed arches, sending a jolt straight to my sex.

"You have beautiful feet. Surprisingly small and dainty despite your stature," he purred as he rubbed his thumbs up and down my inner soles.

"Thank you," I murmured, too caught up with the erotic foot massage to say more. Shoe salesmen were always surprised that I wore a size 6.5AA despite my five foot seven inch height and hearty bone structure.

His thumbs continued making deep circles, sending yet another rush of toe-curling tingles to my core. A moan escaped my throat.

"You like having your feet massaged, don't you?"

I was too enraptured to say a word. I merely nodded.

"Do you know why?"

"Why?" I spluttered.

"Because it releases you. Did you know that the nerves of the feet are connected to various parts of the body? Reflexologists believe that you can turn a woman on with just a foot massage. Even make her come."

He definitely knew what turned on women. At least me. From aphrodisiacs to erogenous zones.

He applied pressure again to that particularly sensitive part of my soles. "Tell me. Where do you feel that?" He pressed deeper.

Oh my God! My core was throbbing. And I could feel wetness pooling along the folds. I swear if he continued with this erotic foot massage, I *was* going to come.

"Answer me, Gloria."

"Between my legs," I moaned.

"Your pussy?"

I nodded.

"Say it, Gloria. 'My pussy.'"

"My pussy," I muttered.

"Good, Gloria. Another 'A' for you." Ending the foot massage with a sensuous kiss on each sole, he unhooked my garters, one by one. My flesh tingled as I felt him peel off my stockings, sensually sliding them down my legs. With a whoosh, the lace garter came off next and then my bikinis.

A dose of reality hit me like a brick. Holy shit! I was laying butt naked on his conference room table. Me, one of the most powerful women in the world, completely at the mercy of a man I hardly knew. Totally exposed and vulnerable. Something was wrong with this picture. What on earth was I doing? *I need to stop this! Collect myself and get the hell out of here!* But I couldn't will myself to sit up. And when his hand slid under my ankles, it was too late.

"What are you doing?" I shrieked.

"What does it feel like?"

Holy fuck! He was tying me up. With one stocking, he bound my ankles together, so tight it almost hurt. And then with the other, he bound my wrists. I attempted to wriggle myself free; it was an exercise in futility. Blindfolded and bound, I was now his prisoner. My heart thudded in my ear, and I was breathing heavily. Now what was he going to do? God, I wished I could see.

"Gloria, now you're mine," he said, his voice deep

and sultry. "I want you to relax. To not be afraid and trust me."

Relax? He wanted me to relax? I was totally bared, tied up, and blinded, and he was about to plunder me. My mind flashed back to what he said in the steam shower the other day. *I'm going to fuck you until you can't walk.* A deep shudder ran through me. I inhaled and exhaled deeply, remembering a breathing lesson from my yoga instructor. I inhaled again, blowing out the air. It wasn't helping.

I shivered again as his warm, velvety tongue slivered up my right leg, from my ankles to the apex. He repeated the action with my other leg, this time leaving it where my inner thigh met the triangle between my legs. Spreading my legs a little, he seamlessly moved his tongue to my cleft, lapping the wet folds like a child lapping a melting popsicle. I moaned as heat rushed to my core. Then, I felt his luscious mouth come down on me, sucking and nibbling. Writhing, I moaned loudly as he rubbed my clit with his fingers. Two? Three?

"Oh, angel, you're so hot and wet. And you taste so good," he said breathily, taking a short respite from his sucking and licking. "I think you're ready."

In two quick moves, he unbound my feet and freed my wrists. I wiggled my limbs while his hand clenched my pussy. I wanted to scream.

"Ms. Long," he said, his voice again businesslike, "you're free to leave. Sit up, and I'll take off your blindfold though I suppose you could do that all by yourself."

I didn't budge. He squeezed my pussy tighter. I groaned.

"Don't you want to leave?"

Go, Gloria, a voice inside my head whispered. My body shouted something else: *I want more!* I shook my head feverishly, from side to side. I was aching for him.

Jaime let out a deep sexy chortle. "I didn't think so. Now, we're going to finish what we started the other day. Spread your legs wide and then bend your knees."

I did as he asked.

"Good girl."

I heard him unzip his slacks and climb onto the table—my sense, kneeling between my steepled legs. He grabbed one of my liberated hands and put it to his shaft. Its heat penetrated my palm and it was already hard. I curled my fingers around the thick, slab of hot velvet, and despite the blindfold, I could envision it in its full glory.

"Gloria, I want you to put my cock inside you." He squeezed my sex again. "If that's what you want. You're the client. The client always comes first."

"Yes!" I gasped.

"Do it!" he ordered.

Blinded, I grappled a little until his erection was perfectly positioned at my hungry opening. Inch by thick inch, I inserted it. To my surprise, I took my time to savor the delicious sensation of my pussy stretching to accommodate his thickening magnificence. When it was almost buried to the hilt, he gave his cock a forceful thrust and just held it there. I clenched my inner muscles around his girth and wondered: did it feel as good for him as it did for me?

"Fucking perfection!" he moaned.

I got my answer. It was perfection...my pussy hugging his cock the way a good-fitting bra hugs a boob. His fullness felt divine.

"Now, I'm going to fuck you."

Yes, fuck me. Fuck me hard. I'm ready!

Gripping my hips, he dragged his shaft back down and then thrust it back up. My drenched walls enabled him to glide smoothly. He repeated the movements, first slowly and then gradually picking up his pace. With each thrust, he hit an unknown sweet spot deep inside me that made me want to weep with carnal pleasure.

"Gloria's spot...the G-spot." He laughed at his own cleverness and then hit it again and again, rubbing against my clit with each masterful stroke.

All I could focus on was the exquisite swelling inside me. Oh, God! What this man was doing to me! He *was* a fucking genius. Pun intended.

I wanted to scream with joy, but bit my lip hard to stifle a shriek.

"Don't worry. The room is soundproof. I always safeguard my interactions with clients. They're highly confidential."

An unnerving thought ran through my head— how many other clients had he fucked right here on this table? Vivien?

"Besides, I want to hear you. Don't hold back."

His intense pounding hurled me back into the moment. We got into a rhythm, my hips rocking to meet his thrusts. Deprived of my vision, my ears took in his harsh breathing and the sound of my beads jiggling against my heaving chest.

The delicious pressure was building, the blindfold heightening the erotic sensations I was feeling. "Oh, God," I heard myself cry out. My nails dug so deeply into the surface of the table I was sure they'd leave marks. I didn't know how much more I could take. I was falling apart.

"Come for me!" ordered Jaime. "Now!" he barked with a harsh thrust and pinch of my clit.

With a long moan, I let go. Waves of ecstasy began to roll through my body. I was coming. Endlessly coming. The waves traveled from my head to my toes. It was like every cell in my body was being taken out to sea. With yet another deep thrust and a loud feral grunt, Jaime spasmed inside me, blasting his hot release as I blissfully rode out my orgasm.

Folding the weight of his body onto me, he crushed my breasts and yanked off his tie from my eyes. I blinked only once, taking in his expression. It was the face of a man who had just won my cunt—skin glazed, eyes hooded, mouth sated.

His breathing stabilizing, he nuzzled my neck, in the very sensitive crook beneath my chin. "Next time, angel, you're going to watch me come." His voice was a sexy rasp.

I wasn't sure about a "next time." I was dazed, confused, wasted; I'd never had such a mind-blowing orgasm. I took in a deep breath to bring air to my brain.

"I've got to go."

"What do you mean? I thought we'd celebrate with dinner. And besides you still owe me." He shot me that sexy smirk.

"I can't. I'm flying back to LA tonight."

He played with my mussed up braid, brushing the wispy ends across my sweat-beaded skin. "I don't want you to go." Sweetness laced his voice.

"I'm sorry. But I've got to. Would you kindly let me get dressed?"

"Fuck. I was ready to bang you again against a wall." He reluctantly rolled off me and dismounted the table.

Sitting at the edge, I watched as he tucked his still semi-hard erection into his slacks. I was still in shock that I'd let this man fuck me on this table and that I'd loved every minute of his assault. Still throbbing, I reached for my undergarments that were strewn on one of the conference table chairs.

His hands got there first. "Let me have the honors. I always cater to my clients." A roguish glint flickered in his eyes.

A shiver tickled my spine as he pulled up my panties and garter. He smiled as the garments made their ascent up my long legs.

"Lift up your beautiful ass."

Anchoring my hands on the table, I raised myself a few inches so that he could get the lacy confections over my butt.

Next the silk stockings.

"Your skin is like satin," he purred as he slinked them up my legs.

My flesh tingled. He expertly rehooked them mid thigh to the garters. I didn't think I'd ever be able to put on another pair of silk stockings without thinking back to this encounter.

He collected my bra. "Slip your hands in," he said with a slight jerk of his chin, holding it up by

the straps. I did as bid, and he slid the bra up my
bare arms. My tender breasts fell into the cups, my
swollen nipples peeking through the lace. His index
fingers circled them before moving to hook the back
clasp. I stifled a moan as a soft smile played on his
face. Next my blouse. His dexterous hands skimmed
my chest as he buttoned it up. This time the moan
escaped.

Lifting me off the table to my feet, he instructed
me to step into my skirt and then shimmied it up to
my waist where he zipped and buttoned it. Lastly,
he helped me into my suit jacket and adjusted my
beads so that they lay perfectly over my collarbone.
There was something adoring in the way he dressed
me. He made me feel taken care of, though not
helpless. It made me want to run my hands along
his gorgeous face, but I refrained.

"Hold on to my shoulders," he said sweetly as he
slipped my Louboutins back onto my feet, where it
had all started. The six-inch fuck me shoes made us
once again face-to-face.

I was back to being me...albeit a just fucked one.
Wobbling, I collected my purse and briefcase. It was
back to business.

"Mr. Zander, don't forget to have your business
affairs people call mine next week. We're going to
have figure out a budget and timeline. I want to
move quickly."

His eyes bore into mine. "Please tell your business
affairs people there's only one deal breaker."

I shot him a puzzled look. "Which would be..."

"I want you to be the point person. Only you, No
one else."

Well, at least, that solved the problem of Vivien. I agreed.

With a satisfied smile, he coiled my braid around his hand. "Ms. Long, I'm looking forward to working with you. We'll make a great team."

His lips smashed into mine. I melted.

"One other deal point. You must always wear red lipstick. It becomes you."

Yeah, he was a genius. A total fucking genius.

Chapter 11

BY THE TIME I WAS back in my hotel room, I regretted what had transpired between Jaime and me. I threw myself into packing my belongings, trying to forget, but the throbbing between my legs and the thudding of my heart made it impossible.

What the fuck had I gotten myself into? I made it a point never to mix business with pleasure and now I had crossed the line big time. I had let this impossible man fuck me. Right on his conference room table! How the hell were we going to work together? This was so fucked.

As I folded up my red bandeau bathing suit, other memories of this week whirled around in my head. Our first encounter on the elevator...our first meeting...the Gloria's Secret Fashion Show...the after-party...our dinners...our swim...the pitch. A wistful smile—and a tingle—accompanied the flashbacks, and then I mentally kicked myself. Why the hell did I let him do the things he did? How could I—this supposedly powerful, in control, respected woman—be so submissive? So taken? No man had ever done this to me before. And it wasn't just his breathtaking looks and his sexual prowess, though that counted for a lot. I was irresistibly drawn to his cocky, confident personality and his outrageous creativity. His brilliance. I'd never met a man like him. He challenged me. He made me fall apart and then put me back together—making me feel more complete, more alive, than I'd ever felt.

Confession: I hadn't taken a shower. Yes, a little gross, but I wanted to wear the essence of him for as long as I could. Given the three thousand or so miles that separated us and the Internet that connected us, it was unlikely that we'd see each other again soon. As I latched the last of my Louis Vuitton travel trunks, I longed for him to knock down the door and fuck my brains out on it. Damn it! He had me bad.

With a disconcerted heart, I called the front desk to have someone collect my mountain of LV luggage. The one thing I was not was a light packer.

The valet came promptly. I followed him to the elevators, my bags piled high on his dolly. I was so hoping, when the elevator doors parted, Jaime would be there, his cocky smile and those sexy denim blues in my face. Ready to take me in his arms and consume my lips with his. Wishful thinking. As the express car descended to the lobby, our first awkward encounter in this elevator replayed in my head. The moment his eyes held mine had been the beginning. And then our fingers touched—a spark of electricity. I shuddered; I could still feel it. Was Madame Paulette right? Was it love at first sight? With a heavy sigh, I wondered: had it been the same for him?

When we reached the lobby and the doors parted, my reverie ended and reality set in. I was going back to Los Angeles. Back to the hectic but solitary life I led. Kevin was flying back with me on the corporate jet while Vivien was staying behind to get some shopping in over the three day weekend ahead; Monday was President's Day and our office was closed.

Following the valet, who was wheeling my luggage to the hotel entrance, I passed by the bar. Friday night, happy hour. It was packed. "Undercover Lover" was playing in the background. I recognized the Kids in Glass Houses song because we'd once used it in a James Bond-themed Gloria's Secret Fashion Show. My eyes took in the boisterous crowd, and then they grew wide. I stopped dead in my tracks. My heart dropped to the floor. At the end of the bar, facing me was Jaime Zander. And all over him was Vivien Holden, one hand fisting his tousled hair, the other cupping his ass, their mouths interlocked. My blood ran cold. I was right. He was into her. I was just another conquest. Another fuck he could add to his stable.

Jaime's eyes caught my mine, frozen with shock. He broke away from Vivien and sprinted my way. I rushed off, my steps quickening until I was running in my six-inch heels to the entrance of the hotel.

"Wait, Gloria!" I heard him shout.

My insides wrenched at the sound of his voice. I didn't look back. Fuck him! The two words looped around my brain. How could he use me like that to win my account? How stupid could I be? Tears stung my eyes. Thank goodness, Kevin was waiting for me at the entrance.

"Come on, Kev, let's get of here." I hooked my arm in his and pushed him through the revolving glass door.

Outside the hotel, in the semi-circular driveway, Nigel was waiting for us with the town car. My bags had already been stowed away in the trunk. I hopped into the car, with a baffled Kevin following behind me. Nigel closed the door and returned to the car. "Lock the doors!" I yelled to my trusty driver.

Shit! There were at least six cars ahead of us. As we waited in line for the vehicles in front of us to leave, there was a loud rapping on the passenger door window. Jaime! Thank goodness the door was locked. My heart was in a frenzy, and tears stabbed at my eyes.

"Open up!" He pounded against the glass with his fist, and with his other hand, tried to yank open the door. His voice boomed through the tinted glass. I looked away.

"Don't touch the door," I barked at a baffled Kevin.

"Glorious, what's going—"

I cut him off. "I'll explain everything as soon as we get out of here."

He shot me a perplexed look.

Jaime was persistent. He pounded with such ferocity I thought his fist might break through the glass. "Roll down the window, Gloria. I need to talk to you."

I shot him an icy glare, facing him just long enough to let him see a tear escape my eyes.

"Gloria!" he shouted again.

I turned my head away and bit my lip, battling more tears. Finally, the car started to move. Jaime stayed with it. Damn him! Was he going to run down Park Avenue with us?

"Nigel, step on it!" I ordered.

"Yes, ma'am." He floored the gas pedal, leaving Jaime behind after one final, frustrated thrust of his fist on the glass pane. I heard him curse as we zoomed off. In no time, we were cruising down the wide city street. I spun my head around and could see Jaime still standing motionless on the corner of Fifty-Ninth and Park.

A golf-ball-sized lump swelled in my throat. Tears, I'd been holding back, streamed down my cheeks.

"Glorious, what's wrong?" asked Kevin, brushing them away.

"Everything. Fucking everything."

By the time we arrived at Teterboro, the nearby New Jersey airport that catered to corporate jets and private celebrity planes, I'd spilled everything to Kevin. He had listened intently, only stopping me with a question or two. Few things shocked Kevin; today's events were among them.

"Shit! This is fucked. Maybe we should move forward with a different agency. We haven't signed a contract."

That wasn't an option. The ZAP! pitch was perfect. It would take weeks, maybe months to find another agency that could come up with a campaign that was as good—if that was even possible. And in the retail business, the longer you waited, the more likely your competition would jump in ahead of you.

"Listen, Glorious. He's on the East Coast; you're on the West. There's three thousand plus miles between the two of you. You never have to physically see him again. Everything can be done through e-mails and an occasional Skype. If someone has to oversee the shoot from our side, I can do that."

I sighed with relief. Kevin was my problem solver. He always had been and always would be. I gave him a hug. I loved him to pieces. We would always be there for each other.

"What about Vivien?" I asked.

"Don't worry about the little minx. I'll handle her."

By the time we arrived at the airport, I was feeling much better. Except for better and for worse, I couldn't get Jaime Zander out of my head.

I braced myself for takeoff. The Gloria's Secret corporate jet was next in line. My stomach bubbled with nerves. I squeezed Kevin's hand. I was petrified of flying, especially takeoffs and landings. Flying made me feel so out of control. My life was totally in the hands of others. The pilot's. And God's. Unfortunately, I spent a good part of my life up in the air, traveling frequently for business meetings around the world. You would think the more I flew, the easier it would get, but it didn't work that way.

Once the plane was up in the air and cruising smoothly, my pulse rate calmed down, and the butterflies in my stomach disappeared. A glass of chilled Chardonnay, served by one of the flight attendants, further relaxed me. By the time I finished it, I was sleepy and shifted my roomy pink leather chair into a reclining position.

"Wake me, when we land in LA," I told Kevin who was watching an episode of *Queer as Folk* on his iPad.

"Sure." He gave me a light peck on my cheek.

I closed my eyes, willing my mind to let go of Jaime Zander. The ache in my heart, however, lingered until sleep took over.

Six hours later, an announcement from our captain awakened me with a startle. It was time to return our chairs to an upright position as we were beginning our descent into Los Angeles. Kevin had dozed off too. We simultaneously raised our chairs.

"Home sweet home," sighed Kevin, who loved sunny Los Angeles as much as I did. It was almost midnight on the West Coast. I gazed out the window at the myriad of twinkling lights below and smiled. Neither of us had known when we'd fled to the City of Angels how much we would fall in love with the sun-kissed weather, the Pacific Ocean, the Spanish architecture, and the colorful, multi-ethnic neighborhoods.

As the plane swooped down, my fear of flying once again took hold of me. My stomach fluttered and my chest tightened. Gripping my hand, Kevin comforted me. "Hold on, Glorious. We're almost there."

I breathed a deep sigh of relief as the plane touched down on the tarmac. Home! We were safely home. I immediately turned my cell phone back on.

There were a dozen phone calls waiting for me from a private number. When I saw the equal number of texts, I knew they were from Jaime.

I read the first text.

Call me as soon as u land.

And then the second.

I can explain.

I didn't need to read the rest. Nor did I have to play his messages. The last thing I wanted was to hear his voice. My body tensed. Pain propelled my rapid heartbeat.

As we pulled into the terminal, the phone rang again. Again a private number. I ignored it. The phone rang again.

"It's him." I clenched my teeth and looked at Kevin beseechingly. "Kev, will you answer it?"

Kevin clutched the phone and put it to his diamond-studded ear. A somber expression washed over his face. "Hold on, please." His long-lashed eyes took in mine. "Glorious, you need to take this call." He handed me the phone.

The phone shook in my trembling hand. I could feel my blood drain from me as I listened to a familiar voice on the other side.

It was Nurse Perez from the Cadbury House for Assisted Living. Madame Paulette was dead. She had died peacefully in her sleep.

My body froze over. I could only feel the scorching tears that poured down my face.

"It's Madame Paulette," I spluttered.

I needed to say no more. Kevin took me into his arms and let me cry on his shoulder. He knew what Madame had meant to me.

"Oh, Glorious, I'm so, so sorry," he soothed as I heaved against him.

The plane refueled. Without ever leaving the cabin, we did an about face, heading back to New York. Collecting myself, I told Kevin about Madame Paulette's wish to be buried next to her late husband in Paris.

"Glorious, I'll arrange for her body to be properly flown to Paris. I'm pretty sure Sandrine, our Paris store manager, is Jewish. I'll contact her to see if she can help with the funeral arrangements."

Thank goodness for my beloved Kevin. Indeed, Sandrine, a good friend, was Jewish. My mind was in a thick fog. What would I do without Kev?

"Do you want me to come to Paris with you?" he asked.

A ghost of a smile flickered on my face; Kevin was always there for me. But this time, I needed to be alone. As soon as he debarked the plane in New York, I was flying solo to Paris.

Chapter 12

I ARRIVED IN PARIS ON SATURDAY a little after eight p.m. I was exhausted, totally jetlagged. Though we fortunately didn't encounter any turbulence during the seven-hour flight from New York, the turbulent memories of the last twenty-four hours rocked my body and mind, making sleep impossible.

As soon as we touched down at Le Bourget airport, I got a text from Kevin. Madame Paulette's body was being flown to Paris, and Sandrine had managed to set up a Jewish burial service the next day, Sunday, at the cemetery where her husband Henri was laid to rest. The driver Kevin had arranged for met me on the tarmac and whisked me off in his limo to The Intercontinental Hotel where I was staying. Like Madame Paulette, I loved Paris. As the Eiffel Tower came into view, a pang of sadness stabbed at my heart. This time, my love affair with the City of Light might end.

Bleary eyed, I checked into the hotel with just a couple of bags as I planned to head back to Los Angeles on Monday after Madame Paulette's funeral.

Having stayed at The Intercontinental numerous times, I was treated with the utmost respect, the staff working quickly to get me into my suite. All I wanted to do was snuggle under fluffy covers and sleep. I couldn't even see straight. As I followed the valet through the bustling opulent lobby to the elevator, a stocky man wearing a long black trench coat and wide brimmed hat that hid his face brushed by me, almost knocking me over.

"*Izvinite,*" he muttered gruffly without slowing down.

It was Russian for "excuse me." A chill ran through me at the thought of Boris Borofsky. I pivoted my head, but the rude man, whose back was now to me, was almost at the front entrance. I took a calming breath. I was tired. It couldn't be him. My mind was just playing tricks on me.

Five minutes later, I was in my beautiful suite, with its plush four-poster canopy bed and regal French furnishings. I quickly shed my clothing, my lingerie the last to go. I could still smell Jaime Zander on me. The memory of him ravaging me on his conference room table replayed in my head. And then the sight of him kissing Vivien kicked that memory out of the ballpark. A mixture of rage and self-loathing coursed through my veins. I shoved all of my undergarments into the waste can by the sink, and then hopped into the shower to wash away the memory of this deceitful man. No matter how hard I scrubbed, his face lingered in my mind.

I towel dried and readied myself for bed, slipping into Gloria's Secret iconic pink and white striped cotton PJ's—made for sweet dreams. *Enfin!* I crawled into the luxurious duvet-covered bed and turned off the light. Unconsciously, I rubbed my fingers over my scar as tears leaked from my eyes. The words of my beloved Madame Paulette swirled around in my head. *It eez better to have loved and lost than never to have loved at all.* In my heart, I mourned the loss of my cherished mentor and scorned the loss of Jaime Zander. My heavy, teary eyes couldn't fight gravity. At last, sleep triumphed over sorrow, but sweet dreams were not to be had.

My wake-up call sounded at six forty-five the next morning. As in any hotel I stayed at, a subsequent knock at my door, signaling the arrival of my coffee, forced me out of bed. I was groggy, a victim of a restless toss and turn sleep and jetlag. After unlocking the door, a jovial mustached waiter set a tray with a pot of steaming coffee along with a pitcher of steamed milk on a small table. It was a welcome blessing.

After draining the strong café au lait, my mind re-activated. I wasn't looking forward to the sad day ahead. A long, hot shower followed. Under the pounding water, I plotted what I was going to wear to Madame's burial. I wanted to look elegant and dignified; I owed her that.

Rifling through my neatly packed Louis Vuitton garment bag, I came upon the perfect black dress— an almost knee-length Dior with a scooped neckline and three-quarter length sleeves. It was one of my favorites and I was glad that I'd packed it. From my other suitcase, a piece of matching luggage, I pulled out my one-piece black lace merrywidow, designed with an underwire and adjustable garters, and the matching v-string panty. After donning the undergarments, I ferreted through the pocket of the suitcase for a pair of black silk seamed stockings. The ones I settled on were my lucky stockings—I took them everywhere I flew, believing their magical powers could protect me from danger, especially a fatal accident. They came from Paris. Madame Paulette had bestowed them upon me on my eighteenth birthday—the first of many pairs she would send me in the years to come. As I carefully rolled them up my legs, I heard her deep raspy voice. "Love *eez* like a fine pair of silk stockings, *ma chérie*. One snag and it can all unravel."

The image of Jaime Zander crept back into my mind. Grabbing my purse and an overcoat, I slumped out of the room, tears threatening to fall.

The cemetery where Madame Paulette was being buried was located on the outskirts of Paris. Tombstones with both crosses and Stars of David dotted the verdant pasture; many dated back to the nineteenth century. A kindly-looking rabbi, with a graying beard and a skullcap, met me at the gravesite and introduced himself. Rabbi Rosenberg. As he took both of my gloved hands in his, my eyes darted to the tombstone of Henri Lévy. My French was good enough to understand the epitaph beneath the etched Jewish star: "Noble hero and devoted husband of Paulette Lévy." Soon his beloved would be by his side again. A chill in the air shot through me.

"She was a special woman, beautiful both inside and out," the rabbi told me. He spoke perfect English. "I knew her well."

I was surprised the rabbi knew her and asked how. It turned out that Madame Paulette attended Shabbat services at his synagogue on Friday nights on her buying trips to Paris.

"She spoke highly about you. You were like a daughter to her."

"Merci," I said in French, tears welling in my eyes. From the corner of one of them, I saw a dozen or so men transporting her casket toward us. My breath caught in my throat.

"A *minyan* from our congregation," said the rabbi, knowing I wasn't Jewish. "They will help us bury her in her final resting place."

The men laid the casket on the grass beside the tombstone of Henri. It was made of pinewood and in the center was a carved Jewish star. It was pure understated elegance —just like her.

One of the men, who was carrying a shovel, began to dig into the earth. They took turns shoveling until a hole that was big and deep enough was made. Using a pulley system, they worked together to lower the casket into it. Then, as the rabbi prayed in Hebrew, each took a turn with the shovel, refilling the hole. I fought back tears as I watched the casket disappear from sight and the large hole fill in. Warm memories of our years together floated in my head along with our final day together. A member of the *minyan* offered me the shovel to cover her with the last mound of dirt. As I scooped up the soil and hurled it onto the grave, the dam holding back my tears burst. The rabbi's melodic Hebrew saturated my mind and soul. I recognized the prayer—The Kiddush. Madame would recite it once a year on the eve of Yom Kippur over the memorial candle that burnt for Henri through the night. The final words, *Oh say, Shalom, Amen,* echoed in my ears. Peace. Rivulets streamed down my face. Madame Paulette was gone...now, in her final resting place...reunited with the man she loved.

I squatted down and retrieved the bouquet of flowers I had brought along—long stemmed white roses—Madame's favorite blooms. I gently laid several on her grave and the remainder against the tombstone of her husband. *Au revoir, Madame.* May you rest in peace and with your true love.

I returned to the hotel, drained and exhausted. It was mid-afternoon.

Before heading up to my room for a much needed nap, I made a stop at the bar. Perhaps, a drink would quell the sorrow that filled my soul. Unable to find an empty table, I settled in at the crowded bar. An international mix of beautiful people, on the make, surrounded me.

Usually just a wine drinker, I ordered something stronger from the young, twinkly-eyed bartender. A vodka martini with extra olives. The very drink I'd ordered with Jaime at the Gloria's Secret after-party. The drink arrived quickly. The cold velvety liquid washed down my throat and was soothing. Just what I needed. The images of Madame Paulette and Jaime Zander faded in my head. I amused myself by observing the eclectic mix of movers and shakers.

Half way through my martini, I felt a warm breath

on the nape of my neck. A familiar voice sent a chill spiraling down my spine.

"Why, Gloria. How uncanny! We meet again."

I spun around, almost knocking over the remains of my drink. Victor!

He was wearing one of his custom-tailored three-piece slate gray suits. In his hand was a tumbler filled with his favorite drink. Bourbon. I knew because I recognized the rancid smell on his breath.

He leaned in close to me. "So, Gloria, what brings you to Paris?"

"Personal business." He had no need to know. "What about you?"

"Business. Pure business. I'm meeting here with someone whose global organization could be a potential strategic partner. If the meeting is successful, I'll invite him to LA to meet you."

Dealmaker Victor was always looking for ways to expand Gloria's Secret. While GS was not the only retailer in Victor's vast empire, it was his most profitable. The more money Gloria's Secret made, the more money Victor made.

He chugged his cocktail and ordered one more. "Can I get you another drink?" he asked, pressing his thigh against mine.

He was making my skin crawl. I edged away from him and shook my head. "I'm fine, thank you." What I really wanted to say was: "Get lost, you prick." I began thinking of a way to excuse myself.

He hovered next to me, nauseating me with his foul bourbon and tobacco-tainted breath. His steely eyes glared into mine. "So, Gloria, I understand from my daughter that you're hiring Jaime Zander and his agency ZAP! to take over advertising."

"Yes." I nodded.

His gunmetal eyes narrowed. "I don't think that's a good idea. I want you to reconsider."

Still sober, I just couldn't believe he was still mad at Jaime for outbidding him on Rihanna's diamond-studded underwear.

"I believe his advertising campaign will bring us to new heights," I retorted. This was the truth, regardless of how much Jaime's deceit had hurt me. At the moment, I didn't know whom I despised more —Vivien or her father.

His face darkened. "Let me tell you, Gloria. Nothing good will come from your relationship with that dilettante."

As much as I loathed Jaime, he was no amateur when it came to his trade. He was pure brilliance. It was time to stand up for him...and myself.

"Victor, you can control our shareholders, but you can't control my day-to-day decisions as CEO. Gloria's Secret is *my* company, and *I* make those decisions."

He smirked. "You're very sexy when you're defiant." He leaned in close to me, his tight lips descending onto mine.

I jerked away. *The pig!* I forced myself to stay diplomatic. "Good night, Victor. And good luck with your meeting. I'll keep you in the loop with regard to our new advertising campaign. I think you'll like it."

I slammed my martini down on the bar counter, leaving Victor with the tab, and stalked off to my hotel room. I so needed to get some rest.

Once at the door to my suite, I rummaged

through my purse for my card key. Where had I put it? My designer bag was so monstrous it could be anywhere. I kept digging. My fatigue made me all the more frustrated.

"I want you, Gloria."

The familiar drawl made me whirl around. Victor again! The glazed look in his eyes told me he was drunk, and in a breath, he was all over me, his hands groping and squeezing.

"Get off of me, Victor," I pleaded.

"No, darling. It's time you and I got to know each other better."

His muscular body pressed me against the hard slab of my door, and then his mouth crushed mine before I could say another word. Exhausted, I didn't have the strength to fend him off. The more I resisted, the harder he pressed. He wormed his repulsive tongue into my mouth, and grinded his stiff arousal against my middle. The groping and squeezing intensified. I writhed and wanted to scream. Desperately. But his mouth and body held me captive. Painfully, I submitted to his advances. I squeezed my eyes closed, to shut out the ugly sight of him.

"Get your fucking hands off her," growled another familiar voice.

In a nano-second, Victor was sprawled over a bouquet of red roses on the carpeted floor. My eyes found my hero. Jaime Zander! He'd come to my rescue. My rapid heartbeat didn't know whether to slow down or speed up. My emotions were in turmoil.

Victor crawled to his knees. He shot Jaime a glaring look, his eyes filled with cold fury. "Be careful, Zander. Don't fuck with *me*. You were always a problem child. And you still are."

Victor's words rippled through me. He had known Jaime since he was a boy?

Jaime didn't flinch as the older man collected himself and stood up. He plucked out a thorn from his expensive suit jacket.

"Get the hell out of here, Victor." Jaime's voice was at once commanding and threatening.

"I'll be watching your every move," hissed Victor. "And yours too, Gloria." Red with rage, he stomped on the exquisite flowers, crushing the delicate buds. He then staggered down the hall to the elevators and disappeared.

I stared blankly at the tattered roses. Once beautiful, they were now in ruin. Their fragility touched something deep inside me, and tears pricked my eyes. I stood there silently, quivering against the door to my suite. A whirling dervish of emotions and questions assaulted me as my eyes met Jaime's intense gaze.

"Are you okay?" he asked, his voice soft.

I nodded, words failing me in my distraught state.

He placed his strong, beautiful hands on my shoulders. I should have been running away from this man but instead I craved to sink into him. His tender touch made the anger, pain, and confusion of the last twenty-four hours fade.

"I'm sorry about the flowers," I finally managed.

"Don't be. I'll buy you three dozen even more beautiful roses."

His words made my heart flutter. "What are you

doing here?"

He fisted my braid and traced my face with the wispy ends. His denim blue eyes never left mine. "I owe you an explanation. What you saw with Vivien is not what you think."

"What do you mean?" I asked, anger creeping back into my voice. My eyes hadn't lied. Fighting back tears, I turned my head away from him.

He cupped my jaw in his hands and gently turned my head to face him. His eyes bore into mine, and in a heartbeat, his lips consumed mine in a deep, passionate kiss that I couldn't resist. I so wanted and needed it. A rush of heat rose to my core before he pulled away.

"Come on, angel. Let's get the hell out of this place. We need to talk."

I did something I needed to do all day. Against his chest, I sobbed.

Twenty minutes later, we were on the Left Bank, in a small but elegant hotel on the Boulevard Saint-Germain, soaking in a deep copper bathtub with champagne flutes on a tray table, an arm's reach away. I was seated backside to him, my knees bent between his outstretched muscular thighs. The hot, sudsy bath was just what my body and soul craved. The tension that had built up inside me began to melt away as Jaime massaged and washed me. His touch was gentle, treating every part of my body reverently, including my breasts. He softly nuzzled my neck, and after tenderly nibbling my earlobes, he breathed into my ear, "We need to talk...but after

I make love to you, my angel."

The L-word stunned me into silence and submission. My shoulders heaved as he lifted my hips and inserted his cock into me, inch by delicious inch. The fullness of him inside me made me moan with pleasure.

"Oh, Gloria, you feel so fucking good. Work with me and trust me." He slowly slid his length down my center, and when he pushed it back up, I met his thrust, enhancing the pleasure for both of us. He let out a sultry sigh.

He was different with me this time. The strokes were smooth and measured, and his soft lips pressed all over the nape of my neck and upper back. The only restraints were his hands, which gripped my hips. Actually, they were more like anchors than restraints, holding me up and helping me ride him as his glorious cock worked me up and down.

He whispered into my ear. "Play with yourself. It'll make it even better for you." It was a sweet command, not a barking order.

Still gripping a hip and not missing a stroke, he used his spare hand to place my right hand to the soft folds between my inner thighs. His hand stayed on top of mine as he guided it up and down along the sensitive tissue. No stranger to masturbation, I quickly found my clit and circled my fingers around it. His hand returned to my hip and he intensified the grinding between my legs. He was right. Right as usual. I arched my head as the intense pleasure I was giving myself mingled with the extreme pleasure he was giving me. Oh, God! I wanted to come!

"Don't come yet," instructed Jaime, a hint of his

controlling behavior seeping into his sultry voice. "I want to enjoy this for as long as I can."

I didn't know how much longer I could hold on. The waves of ecstasy had begun to roll through my core, the inevitable not far away. My breathing grew ragged with his. Craving my moment of release, I dug the fingernails of my free hand into his thigh as I tried to restrain myself.

"Now, angel," he finally said. "Fall apart for me."

On cue, my whole body shook as my core splintered around his pulsating member. His own orgasm came seconds later with a roar of my name. My head fell back against his taut chest. I could feel it rise and fall, the movements slowing as his breathing stilled. His heartbeat sang in my ear like a love song. He wrapped a brawny arm around my shoulder, coiling my damp braid around his hand, and nuzzled the side of my sensitive neck. His other hand caressed my quivering clit. Bliss. Pure bliss. I don't know how long we stayed in that position when I heard him say, "Gloria, turn around. Face me. We need to talk."

So relaxed, all I wanted to do was stay curled up in his arms and close my eyes. But he was right. We needed to talk, and he had traveled far to have a serious conversation. There were so many burning questions that needed answers. I shifted my body so that my longs legs were spread over his, and we were facing each other. His expression was intense, his lush lips pressed tight, and his blue eyes piercing. He looked anxious. I'd never seen this side of him. My heart pounded with anticipation. Maybe I wasn't going to like what I was about to hear. Taking a deep breath, I braced myself and began.

"How did you know I was here in Paris?"

"Gloria, you should know this about me by now. Where there's a will, there's a way. I had to see you."

"You didn't answer my question," I fired back at him.

"I found out from your PR guy. Are you here on business?"

"Personal business." I wasn't ready to tell him about Madame Paulette. It was all too complicated. And I didn't want to get all choked up. Steeling myself, I instead asked the question that most needed an answer.

"Are you fucking Vivien?" I could have said "involved with Vivien," but it just came out that way. I held my breath waiting for his response.

He sucked in a gulp of air between his teeth.

My heart skipped a beat. *He was!*

He blew out the air. "Vivien is my stepsister."

Dead silence. Shockwaves coursed through my body. I struggled to process the information. Victor's earlier words, "you were always a problem child," echoed in my head. "Victor Holden is your father?"

"No, my stepfather. My mother was his second wife."

With that, Jaime launched into his life story, unconsciously rubbing his thumb over the raised scar that marred my chest.

Jaime's mother, a raven-haired beauty named Delilah, I learned, married his real father, Payton Anthony Zander, a struggling artist, when she found out that she was pregnant with his child. A painter's model, they had met when the young beauty had posed for him. For Payton, it was love at first sight. Eighteen-year-old Delilah was the muse and lover he'd always dreamt about. The child only added to his infatuation.

Unbeknownst to Payton, the beautiful but impoverished Delilah was an opportunist. She'd agreed to marry Payton, not because he'd fathered her child, but because he had the potential to become a billionaire breakout painter in the league of Jackson Pollack. She dreamt of a life of riches and glamour. And he was the gateway. Except life didn't turn out as she'd hoped.

Living in a decrepit loft in Venice Beach, California, the young couple struggled to make ends meet; years went by. Jaime's father remained convinced that each painting would be his first masterpiece, his ticket to fame and fortune. Delilah grew angry and frustrated with Payton's delusions and resented the love child they'd created because it was just another mouth to feed. More desperate to dress in designer clothing than to keep a roof over their heads, she took on a temporary job as the assistant to a mega-wealthy CEO, a recent divorcee. Victor Holden. Her sensual beauty, even at the age of thirty-two, was irresistible. Their relationship blossomed into something more permanent, both professionally and personally. Six months later, Delilah Zander was the next Mrs. Victor Holden. And thirteen-year-old Jaime was living under the roof of their Beverly Hills mansion along with Victor's daughter from his first marriage—Vivien.

"My father was devastated. He never stopped loving my mother. We were his whole world."

His voice hoarse, Jaime took a break to sip some champagne. I followed suit, eager to hear more. I'd already learned so much about him. His father's portrait of him as a baby that hung in his office flashed into my head. His good looks must have stemmed from his beautiful mother and his creative talent from his artistic father, who I suspected was physically attractive as well.

"Why didn't your father fight for custody of you? Even joint-custody?" I asked.

Jaime took another sip of the champagne and set the glass back onto the tray table next to the tub. Pain filled his eyes. His fans of thick lashes lowered. "He didn't have a chance. He was stone broke and stoned out."

I'd seen Jaime cocky-confident and I'd seen him angry-mad. But sad was something new. I ran my fingers through his silky, damp hair and met his forlorn eyes. I could feel them reach out to me. He inhaled a deep breath.

"Three months after my mother married Victor, my father took his life. He shot himself."

With a gasp, I clapped a hand to my mouth. The explosive sound of a gunshot filled my head. Reliving my own gunshot, I shuddered.

Jaime tenderly cupped my face between his hands. "Are you okay?"

Returning to the moment, I nodded. I now understood what made Jaime Zander who he was. Why he needed money, power, and control. He was afraid of falling into a dark abyss in the footsteps of his poor, struggling father. By controlling women and shunning commitment, he could avoid being hurt the way his father had been by his mother. I also understood why he hated Victor Holden. Victor had destroyed his parents' marriage and brought his father to the ultimate jumping off point of despair.

"Were you close to your father?" I asked softly, suspecting the answer.

"Very. Even with his downfalls. He was loving. Creative. Fun. He taught me to open my eyes and see the world. To use my imagination. I was a lot like him."

The look on Jaime's face grew melancholic. In his mind, he was traveling back in time. Reliving nostalgic memories with his beloved father.

A pang of sadness shot through me. It wasn't hard for me to imagine how difficult it was for a beautiful, confused thirteen-year-old boy to lose his father, the person he loved the most in the world. Kevin, in a way, had gone through that tragic journey with his homophobic father; a different kind of loss, but nonetheless the loss of a cherished parent.

I gently rubbed my hand along the side of his face, relishing the soft layer of unshaven stubble. "I'm sorry about your loss."

Jaime quirked a ghost of a smile. "My father's always been my inspiration. A day doesn't go by without thinking about him. I still miss him."

I now saw Jaime differently. Behind the confident, cocky façade was a sensitive, wounded soul. With my own narcissistic, negligent mother and broken childhood, there was a new, profound connection between us. I circled his face lightly with my fingertips. Though I already knew the answer, I asked, "Do you blame Victor for destroying your father?"

Jaime stiffened. His eyes blazed with fury. "I blame him for destroying my father *and* my mother." He paused. *"And* for almost destroying me."

My eyes widened. "What do you mean?"

"He abused me."

The web of fine scars along his back flickered in my head. He was being opened, so I dared to ask him, "Did Victor physically hurt you?"

Jaime's blue eyes narrowed and his lips clenched. He sucked in a sharp breath. "The bastard beat me. He liked using his riding crop."

"Oh my God," I cried out. My loathing for Victor spiked and consumed me. A mixture of rage and sorrow coursed through my blood. I had the burning urge to run my lips over every one of Jaime's scars. I'd read once that scars tell you the hurt is over. That you've healed. That was pure bullshit. They always reminded of you the past and the pain. My own above my heart never stopped.

Jaime continued. "Victor hated me. I was just something in the way. And I was not his blood... unlike Vivien who he adored."

Vivien. The sound of her name made me cringe. "How old was Vivien when you moved to Victor's house?" I asked.

"Twelve going on twenty."

I did the math in my head. That meant she was older than the twenty-nine years she claimed to be; in fact, we were probably the same age. *The lying bitch!*

"How did you and Vivien get along?"

"Vivien was a manipulative, spoiled brat who had

a crush on me. I was a vulnerable, insecure, fucked up kid. One night when she was fifteen, she raided her father's liquor cabinet, and we both got drunk."

I knew what was coming next and braced myself.

"She got me to fuck her."

I inhaled air through my nose. "Do *you* still fuck her?"

"No, but she still wants to fuck me. What you saw at the bar was another one of her manipulative attempts to get me into bed. I was trying to ward her off without creating too much of a scene when you passed by."

Deep inside, I knew he was telling the truth. I lowered my eyelids, suddenly feeling bad that I'd mistrusted him. "I'm sorry I ran off." My voice was small.

Jaime tilted up my chin and gazed into my eyes. "Angel, you don't have to apologize. You had no idea." He paused. "There's something else you need to know. Vivien's not my type. I could never be with her. She's a dominatrix."

The news of Vivien's sexual preference didn't surprise me, given her brazen personality and fashion sense. In my head, I could easily imagine her in a black leather corset, fishnet stockings, and thigh-high leather boots, wielding a whip. Victor's riding crop? Had she ever used it on Jaime? I inwardly shuddered; I didn't want to know.

Jaime toyed with my wet braid. "You understand now, why I can't work with her on the account. She's a force, however, that must be reckoned with. She's potentially dangerous and destructive."

I mulled over his words. The situation was

complicated. I was going to have to figure out a way to keep Jaime away from Vivien. And also from Victor.

An afterthought flew into my head. I knew that Victor was now single and never talked about Jaime's mother. I recalled Jaime telling me he'd inherited a lot of money from her. Had she died?

"What happened to your mother?" I asked.

"Five years after Victor married my mother, he had an affair with a young starlet and asked for a divorce. My mother was more angry than heartbroken and, in the end, went for a large settlement, that included a mansion in Bel Air. No longer the beauty she used to be, she resorted to alcohol and sedatives. Driving under the influence, she died the day before she turned forty in a head-on collision on the canyon road that led to our house."

So, in a way, Victor had destroyed Jaime's mother's life as well. Jaime's tragic past tugged at my heartstrings. I felt connected to him in a way that I could never have imagined. He was a tortured soul just like me. Deprived of maternal love. And that of a father who adored him. I had just one last question.

I looked him straight into the eye. "Jaime, why did you wait so long to tell me all this?" So many complicated conflicts of interest could have been avoided had I known about his toxic connection to Victor and Vivien.

He did that swirly thing with my braid again and then tickled my lips with the ends. "Because..." His voice trailed off.

"Because why?" I said softly, his intense gaze

arousing me.

"Because I wanted to work with you, Gloria. From the minute I read about you online, I was drawn to you. Your success, your drive, your own need for control. And when I met you in the elevator, I was so taken by your beauty, feistiness, and independence. The need to control you consumed me. You're different from all the women I've been with. You're brilliant, intoxicating, and infuriating. You inspire and excite me, and sometimes you even make me lose control." He tugged hard at my braid and shot me a wry smile. "And because, Ms. Long...I'm crazy about you."

"Mr. Zander, you make me crazy!" *Crazy in love?* I wasn't sure because I really didn't know first hand what that meant. Feeling tingles everywhere? Shortness of breath? Fiery desire? Jealousy? A sense of loss when the other person is not there? That's what my book heroines felt. And I felt all those things too.

I laughed. For sure, some kind of defense mechanism.

"Get over here, you!" he ordered, his eyes dancing with mischief. He wrapped his sculpted arms around me. With one swift smooth move, he hauled me against him and drove his rigid cock into me. My forehead fell to his shoulder as he nibbled at my soaked flesh and ravaged my soaked core. He held me tightly, helping meet his deep thrusts. I moaned with pleasure. My arms clasped his chiseled body, embracing the scars that lined his back. He groaned my name. As this beautiful, controlling, complex man brought me to yet another earth-shattering climax, I was too distracted to think of all the complications he was bringing into my life.

We were both so exhausted. Jaime was still on East Coast time, and I truthfully didn't know what time zone I was in. I just knew I was zoned out.

After room service, a light supper consisting of a delicious Salade Niçoise and bottle of Pouilly-Fuissé, we decided to called it a night. Jaime, clad in loose blue pajama bottoms that hung sexily low on his narrow hips, insisted on picking out my sleeping attire. The control freak!

My comfy pink and white striped PJ's? Not a chance! Rifling through one of my overnight bags, he found a sheer, lace-trimmed black-and-white polka dot baby doll set from the Gloria's Secret "Irresistible" collection. A diabolical grin whipped across his face upon coming across his treasure. "Perfection!" He expertly dressed me in the sexy sleepwear. It was hard for him to keep his mouth and hands off me, but I didn't mind.

"Which bed?" asked Jaime, admiring his handiwork. "The client gets to pick."

Typical of European boutique hotels, the charmingly furnished floral room had two double beds. I went for the one on the right closest to the French windows. He swept me into his arms and carried me to it, slipping me under the fluffy duvet. He followed me under the covers and snuggled close to my scantily clad body. The warmth of his flesh heated mine.

I rolled over to my side and propped myself up on

my elbow. My eyes soaked in his face. His hooded blue eyes, his lush lips, and the strong angles of his stubble-laced jaw. God, he was gorgeous any way you looked at him. I dusted the tip of my braid across his dimpled chin, fighting off my hot desire to dip my tongue into the kissable indent.

"Mr. Zander, what I meant is...this is my bed. You sleep in the other one. Client's wishes." While we had fucked our brains out, sleeping with him in the same bed was strangely something I wasn't ready for. It felt wrong. Even more so, it scared me.

Resting his head on the mountain of fluffy pillows, he cocked an eyebrow. "Gloria, you've got to be fucking kidding. I flew all the way to Paris to be with you, and you don't want to sleep with me?"

I sat up and folded my arms across my chest. The way his eyes bore into mine was making this difficult. "No," I said before changing my mind. "Go!" I aimed my pointer finger at the other bed.

He shot me that maddening smirk. "So, Ms. Long, before I unfortunately have to leave, can you tell me if I should put this room on my list of client expenses?"

"Stop procrastinating!" I playfully hit his bare chest with one of the pillows. When I thought about it more, I shouldn't have been so frivolous. I was going to have to be extra careful working with Jaime, with his ruthless stepfather, Victor Holden, watching our every move.

"And should I bill time for this?" In a breath, he rolled on top of me, flattening me on the mattress. He smashed his lips against mine, with a fierce kiss that sent a rush of tingles to my core and then slipped his hand beneath my lace-trimmed bottoms. He fingered his way to my clit. I groaned.

"You don't really want me to leave," he breathed into my ear.

Confession: No, I didn't. I was practically on fire. His fingers circled my bud vigorously, bringing me closer to combusting with each rotation. I fisted his silky hair and moaned, "Don't stop."

"Don't worry," he moaned back.

I could feel his cock hardening and elongating, growing thicker and hotter by the second. My body was desperate for him. Consumed with feverish desire, I moved one hand to the waistband of his pajama bottom and fumbled with the drawstring to loosen it.

"Good girl, Gloria," he breathed as he raised his torso just slightly, enabling me to lower his bottoms. My hand skimmed his rock-hard ass. *What an ass!*

"Lift up!" he ordered.

I did as bid, and he pulled down my baby doll bottoms as far as they would go. "I should have just torn them off you," he mumbled under his breath as my feet wiggled out of them.

With a powerful thrust of his knees, he spread my legs wide apart and then plunged his hot, pulsing cock into me. A loud, satisfied sigh met his penetration.

"Oh, angel, you're so wet and ready for me." He anchored his hands on the mattress to support himself and began to pump in and out of me.

"So. Do. You. Still. Want. Me. In. The. Other. Bed?" he grunted with each determined bang.

"No!" I gasped. He was hitting my G-spot

repeatedly. I was falling apart at the seams with ecstasy.

A triumphant smile splayed on his face. "That's what I thought."

He picked up his pace with each long, hard stroke. I gripped his perfect buns of steel, pressing them forward with his thrusts, though, trust me, assistance was the last thing he needed. I just needed something to hold on to—to keep me from leaving this planet. Whimpering and rocking with him, I clenched my eyes. Sparks were flying in my head as my core prepared to burst with out of this world pleasure. *Oh, God!* I was not going to last much longer.

"Gloria, open your eyes. I want you to watch me come."

I did as he asked and drank in the intensity that lusted on his sweat-drenched face. His half-moon eyes sucked me in and his luscious lips parted with pants of desire. His pulsating cock let me know he was on the verge.

"Now!" he shouted. He let out a loud savage sound from deep inside him and arched his head. We climaxed together. His cock exploded while my core lit up like a disco with strobing bright colors. The song "Gloria" played in my head. *Oh, oh, oh, calling Gloria.*

"Oh, Gloria. That was fucking amazing."

Yes, it was. It was fucking amazing.

Catching his breath, he sunk his head into the thick fold of my cleavage. I wrapped one arm around his sweat-soaked body and threaded the fingers of the other through his damp, tousled locks. Closing my eyes, I hummed the melody of "Gloria." All the voices in my head were calling his name.

Repositioned on my back, my head resting on his bare chest, I asked him something that had been on my mind. "Mr. Zander, are you into the whole BDSM lifestyle?"

He chuckled. "No, In fact, I'm not really a dom."

My brows furrowed. "What do you mean?" His controlling behavior mirrored that of many of the erotic book boyfriends I had.

"My shrink says I'm a just a creative control freak with kinky tendencies."

Semantics.

"Do you get off on physically hurting women?" My heartbeat accelerated going into this dangerous territory. Given that his mother had destroyed his beloved father, the psychologist in me thought it was likely though he'd never physically harmed me.

"Whatever way you call it, I'm strictly BD without the SM." He planted a tender kiss on my cheek. "Besides, angel, you're like the lace you wear. Beautiful and fragile, easily torn. I could never hurt you."

Inwardly, I heaved a sigh of relief. I wasn't sure I could put up with the inflicted pain I'd read about in those BDSM novels. I'd already had enough emotional and physical pain in my life. The lace analogy struck a deep chord inside me.

He played with my braid. "So I assume after that mind-blowing fuck it's okay for me to sleep with you." A statement not a question.

"Don't assume anything." *Mr. Presumptuous!* I had to show him that I had some power. That he couldn't always fuck me into submission.

We had a stare-off. His intense denim blues and cocky half smile were wearing me down. God, he was sexy and beautiful! My core was buzzing. I wanted him all over me again. Finally, before I caved in, I said, "If you don't leave this bed, I will."

"You're a tough client." With a roll of his eyes, he climbed out of the bed and nestled into the other one to my left. He turned off the overhead light between us.

"Sweet dreams, Ms. Long."

"Sweet dreams, Mr. Zander," I mimicked before drifting off.

I'm running through a black tunnel. I can see nothing in front of me, nothing behind me. My legs propel me as fast as they can; my lungs burn. My heavy breaths and footsteps pierce the darkness. I can't let him find me. I can't! Suddenly, footsteps thunder behind me. I steal a glance backward; I see nothing, but the footsteps are getting louder and faster; they're gaining on me. I try to run faster, but my legs won't let me.

"Nobody steals from Boris Borofsky!" The accented voice booms behind me. "You will pay!"

"No!" I scream silently. I must escape. Oh God, where is the light? Where is the end? Will I always be on the run?

A deafening blast echoes in the endless chamber of darkness. And then another. A bolt of white light scorches through my body. Red-hot liquid streams down my flesh. I keep running. I must keep running! I can never stop running! Oh the pain!

Screaming, I bolted to an upright position. The hot liquid in my dream was now a rush of cold sweat, and it was pouring out of every crevice of my quaking body. Two strong arms wrapped around my drenched torso and pulled me against a slab of rippled, warm flesh.

"Gloria, what is it? Are you okay?" Jaime's velvety voice filtered into my ear. I let myself sink into him, shuddering against his manly, hard chest. His warmth blanketed me.

I took several deep, calming breaths just like my shrink instructed me to do after one of these mind-shattering dreams. Words, however, stayed trapped in my throat.

Still holding me, Jaime smoothed my damp, matted hair.

"It's okay, angel. I'm here. Why are you shaking?"

I moistened my parched palate with my tongue and found my voice. "It was just a bad dream." *My forever nightmare.*

"Do you want to tell me about it?" His voice was soft and full of compassion.

"I can't." At least right then, I couldn't. I wasn't ready to confide in this man—to tell him my secret. Though he had shared his scars, mine was still my cross alone to bear-with the exceptions of Kevin, who had lived it, and Madame Paulette, who had taken it to her grave.

"Come on, let's go back to sleep." He gently lowered me to the bed, and tucked me back in like a child. He kissed me lightly on the lips before lowering himself next to me.

"I don't think this is a good idea," I whispered.

His beautiful agile fingers traced my face. "Gloria, I'm not going to ravage you. I'm just going to hold you. You need me. Now roll over."

I did as he asked and felt my body cocooned in his. He draped his arms around me, one hand brushing across my scar. My body softened in his as his heartbeat soothed my soul. For the first time in my life, I truly felt safe. There were so many things this gorgeous man could do to me. And needing him right now was one of them.

"Gloria, you've got to learn to trust me. Even with your secrets." He gently kissed my head. "Now, sleep, my angel. I've got a big day planned for us tomorrow."

Spooned in the safe harbor of his arms, I couldn't battle the weight of my heavy eyelids. Before I could tell him that I was heading back to Los Angeles first thing in the morning, sleep took hold of me.

Chapter 13

I WOKE UP IN THE MORNING in the same position I'd fallen asleep. Blinking one sleepy eye open after the other, I glanced at the alarm clock on the night stand—6:05 a.m.—and then cranked my neck to look at the man who was holding me. He was still sound asleep, soft rhythmic breaths emanating from his lush parted lips. Wisps of his sleep-tousled hair tumbled onto his forehead and a layer of fine stubble laced his face. God, he was beautiful in the morning.

Resisting the urge to run my fingers over his fine features, I carefully rolled away from him, hoping not to wake him.

He stirred. "Gloria," he moaned. The breathy way he said my name was like a prayer. He stirred again, but to my relief, his eyes remained shut. A dreamy smile played across his gorgeous face. I wondered—could he be dreaming about me?

I tiptoed over to the luggage rack, where my suitcase was sitting. Rifling through the contents, I found something comfortable to wear on my long flight back to Los Angeles—a pair of Gloria's Secret pink sweats and matching hoodie. I decided to forego underwear. All I wanted to feel was the softness of the fleece against my skin. And the memory of Jaime

Zander's touch everywhere.

I lifted off my baby doll top, stepped out of the matching bikini bottoms, and then folded them neatly into my suitcase. As I reached for the sweats, a breath of hot air descended on my neck and two powerful arms cinched my waist. His bare silky chest brushed against my back. He was up.

"Where do you think you're going, Ms. Long?" Jaime purred. His velvety lips nuzzled the uber-sensitive spot on my neck just below my ear. My skin prickled all over.

I squirmed, trying to break loose of his grip. "I'm going back to LA. My plane departs this morning."

He tightened his grip with one hand, and tugged my disheveled braid with the other. "You're not going anywhere. We're in Paris. I have the whole day planned, and a special treat in store for you this evening."

Special treat? The words sent goose bumps to my skin. I was intrigued and tempted, but I stuck to my guns.

"Really, I've got to get back. I've been out of my office for more than a week."

"Bullshit. Your office is closed today. It's President's Day."

He was right. *Think, Gloria, think.* Except it was hard to think with this god nibbling at my earlobes. A bolt of unexpected erotic pleasure zapped my core. I was heating up.

"I've got a lot of paperwork to do and e-mails to catch up on," I stammered.

"Me too," he breathed into my ear. "We can do them together here. Plus, we can get going on your ad campaign."

I had to get used to the idea that this impossible man and I would be working together. The obstacles ahead—salacious Victor and his predatory daughter Vivien—flew into my head, sending a chill down my spine. And I still wasn't sure how I was going to manage our physical relationship or my emotions. Jaime could feel me tense up; he massaged my shoulders.

"Let me think about it," I managed as he pressed his lips to my shoulder blades and trailed down my spine with deliciously ticklish flutter kisses.

"Angel, don't over think because there's nothing to think about."

I closed my eyes, my mind filled only with the sweet sensation of his kisses. Oh, God! I was melting into him. It took all I had to stay on track.

"Let go of me. I need to get dressed," I pleaded.

He let out a loud, exaggerated sigh. "Oh, Gloria, must I?"

Still clutching me with one arm, he leaned over me and dug his spare hand into my suitcase. He rummaged through my neatly folded garments.

"What the hell are you doing?" I protested.

"Security check. Looking for a dangerous weapon."

What the fuck?

"Bingo!" he exclaimed as he pulled out one of my sheer silk stockings. "You're under arrest."

"Huh?"

Before I could get my mouth to close, he yanked my arms behind my back with such force a painful pull ripped across my shoulder blades. He gripped both my wrists in one hand.

"What are you doing, you crazy asshole?" I cried out, trying impossibly to free myself.

"You're going to pay, my sweet, for calling me that."

I swallowed hard, still writhing.

With his spare hand, he began binding my hands together with the stocking. I felt him tie a tight knot. I couldn't even wiggle my fingers. They were bound together so tightly I was sure my circulation had been cut off.

"Untie me, you bastard! You can't do this to me." I wheeled around. A diabolical smirk played on his gorgeous face. God damn him! He could.

"I'm going to call security," I threatened.

Jaime bent over with laughter. "Oh, so you're going to dial the room phone with your nose?" He lightly flicked the tip of my nose with his thumb. "And then you're going to unlock the door with that talented mouth of yours and let Mr. Security see you tied up and naked?" He playfully traced the outline of my lips.

I screwed up my face.

"You're so cute when you do that."

Damn him!

The ring of my cell phone sounded from inside my handbag.

"I need to get that. It could be some kind of emergency."

The ringing stopped. And then it picked up again.

"Mr. Zander, would you be kind enough to retrieve my phone, press answer, and then put it to my ear."

"Say please."

"Please," I grumbled. "It's in the zipper compartment of my purse."

With a wicked grin, he did as asked. My monstrous bag was parked on the dresser across from the beds. My eyes stayed fixed on him as he strode over to it, soaking in his broad shoulders, rippled back, and boyishly narrow hips. His beauty made his painful scars almost invisible.

He found the phone easily and headed back to me with it in his hand. It kept ringing.

He hovered over me. "Tell whoever it is you're tied up."

That was a fact.

I gazed at the screen. It was Kevin.

Jaime pressed answer and then held the phone to my ear.

"Hi, Kev. Is everything okay?" My voice faltered.

"More than okay. I'm just checking in on you. You sound strange. Are you okay?"

"Yeah. I'm just a little tied up at the moment." *Did I really just say that?*

Jaime rewarded me with a chaste kiss on top of my head.

"Did everything go smoothly with Madame Paulette's funeral?"

"Yes. It was a beautiful service. Thanks so much for helping."

"Say good-bye," Jaime breathed against my neck, his lips skimming my sensitive skin. He simultaneously draped his free arm over my shoulder, crossing my chest until he was groping my tender breasts. He began to massage them. A delicious chill skated down my spine, erasing the sad memory of my beloved Madame Paulette.

"When are you coming back?" asked Kevin.

"Um, uh, tomorrow. I'm going to stay in Paris an extra day."

Jaime rewarded me this time with a squeeze of each nipple. They instantly grew into pointed crowns as he twirled them between his forefinger and thumb. My temperature was rising. He tweaked them again, sending tingles to my core. I moaned into the phone; Kevin heard it.

"Is Jaime there?"

I gulped. I couldn't hide anything from Kevin.

"Yeah."

"Good. He told me about Vivien hitting on him. He's a good guy. Paris is the City of Love. You should let him fuck your brains out."

Kev never held back. Never. "I'm thinking about it."

"Oh, Glorious, I wish you could see me. I'm doing a happy dance."

I could actually picture Kevin doing a little jig. Not wanting to dwell on Jaime, I changed the subject. "And what about you?"

"I'm still in New York…"

"With…"

"Ray. He's fucking amazing."

Holy shit! This entangled business relationship was growing more complicated by the minute. Maybe I should end it.

Jaime nibbled my earlobe. "Say good-bye," he breathed into my ear. "And then say hello to this." He dragged his thick erection along my backside. His heat penetrated my skin, sending embers to the pit of my stomach. Wetness pooled between my legs. Fuck. He was making me lose control again.

"Kev, I've got to go," I stammered.

Kevin let out a laugh. "Don't let me keep you from sightseeing."

The only sightseeing in my near future was the monument between Jaime's legs.

As we exchanged good-byes, Jaime tossed the phone across the room into my open handbag. "Now, spread your legs and bend over," he ordered.

I did as he asked, pressing my head to the soft mattress. My hands remained tied up behind me. They were beginning to go numb.

Standing behind me, Mr. Impossible groped my buttock cheeks and then kneaded them. "This must be the finest view in all of Paris," he purred. "You've got one magnificent ass."

Before I could say a word, he rubbed the head of his cock up and down the crack of my butt. Though I didn't feel much sensation, it was strangely erotic. A hand moved between my thighs, his fingers finding their way to my aching clit. He stroked my sensitive folds and then rubbed circles around my nub. Now, that I felt.

"You're so wet for me, angel."

A muffled moan escaped my throat.

"I'm going to fuck your beautiful ass. Have you ever been fucked this way before?"

"No," I managed with a shake of my head.

"Good. You're going to love it."

He rubbed his cock along my wet folds. It didn't stay there long—just long enough to bathe in my hot juices. His fingers released my clit, and the next thing I knew his hands, one of them warm and wet, were spreading my ass cheeks apart. I felt his hot crown nudging at my opening. I wasn't sure about this. With my head still pressed against the bed, I squeezed my eyes shut. A battle between fear and desire raged in my core. Every muscle in my body tensed.

"Relax, Gloria. This is going to hurt at first, but once I'm inside you're going to wish I never left."

I took a deep breath, preparing myself for his invasion.

He penetrated me and I winced. Then, slowly he began to fill me, sliding his lubricated cock straight to my center. I clenched my weeping pussy. It hurt like hell, but not as much as I thought it would. I kept on taking deep breaths as he stretched me, his warm hands splayed on my hips to hold me steady. When I began to relax, the pain morphed into tortuous pleasure. The fullness of his slick length inside my virgin hole sent a blast of erotic sensations through my body that I wasn't expecting.

"Jesus, you're so hot and tight. Are you okay?"

I simply nodded into the bed. My brain had forgotten how to send words to my voice box. All I could think about was him dominating me this way.

He caressed my ass. "Good, angel. Keep breathing." He slowly withdrew and then pushed forward, again slow and deep. I groaned, growing fonder of the snugness. His pelvic bones slammed against me as he repeated the movement and picked up his pace. Moaning, I found myself rocking back and forth with his thrusts, each one more intense. Each one more divine. The burning fire inside me was making me delirious. I was loving it.

"This will make it even more pleasurable." His fingers moved back to my hungry clit, and he began to rub it vigorously. A scream escaped my throat. His other hand clutched my left buttock cheek, still steadying me as he dragged his length up and down my tender hole.

"Oh, angel," he groaned, his breathing harsh. "You feel fucking incredible. So wet and hot everywhere. How does it feel for you?"

I was fucking losing it. The hot tingles between my legs mingled with the fiery friction of his thrusts. The insane pressure inside me was building like a rockslide. He was doing it again—sending me over a cliff. Making me lose control.

"I'm going to come!" I cried out.

"Not yet!" he barked.

Oh, God. I was so close to the edge. How was I going to hang on? And then a new mind-blowing sensation blew through me. Two slick fingers plunged into my other opening and began sliding up and down my cavity, hitting my hot spot each time. He was finger fucking and butt fucking me in tandem. I began to whimper. I thought I would pass out right on the bed. *Oh, please let me come!*

As I raced toward orgasm, Jaime continued to work me on both ends. His panting accelerated with his relentless thrusts. My body was convulsing. I could hold on no longer. The pressure was so intense that I was actually seeing stars.

"Please!" I pleaded, lifting my head from the bed and twisting it so that I could see his face. His expression was sexy and savage. His tousled hair fell into his hooded eyes; sweat beads dusted his skin, and his parted mouth curved in a dangerous pout. His lustful eyes met mine.

"Now, Gloria. Fall apart, now!" he shouted.

I screamed as everything inside me broke loose. Waves of ecstasy wracked my body, spasm after spasm. He shoved his two fingers and his cock deep inside me one more time, and then with a roar, he climaxed violently inside me. Hot cum seeped into my backside while juices seeped out of my core. His intense vibrations collided with mine. With one more thrust, this one softer, he finished off his orgasm and made me come with fury again. *Holy fuck!*

I buried my head back into the bed as he eased out of me. Damn him. He was right. I was bereft. I missed his fullness already.

He untied my hands, and after wiggling my fingers to bring back sensation, I just let my arms hang lose by the sides of my legs like a rag doll. He ran his warm velvety tongue down my spine and then back up, sending a rush of goose bumps to my already prickling skin.

He gave my ass a playful slap. "You're free to go back to LA now, angel."

I wasn't going anywhere.

Paris was for lovers.

After a delicious, hot shower in which Mr. Controlling fucked Ms. Losing It yet again, we towel dried each other and put on the fluffy terry cloth robes that came with room. Jaime ordered room service. Over scrumptious flakey croissants and steaming cafés au lait that we savored around a small round table, he told me what he had planned for the day. It was going to a leisurely day of strolling in Paris and taking in a few sights and museums. And of course, a stop for lunch and a glass of wine at a neighborhood café. I told him that I wanted to make a stop at our Paris flagship store on the Champs-Elysées in the late afternoon. I wanted to check it out and above all personally thank the store manager, Sandrine—a good friend—for helping me with Madame Paulette's funeral arrangements. That was only yesterday yet it felt like eons ago. A wave of sadness swept over me. I was going to miss her. Jaime readily agreed to the visit, telling me that he had some personal stuff to take care of too, including a client.

"You have a client in Paris?" I asked, arching my brows.

"Angel, I have clients all over the world."

Girlfriends?

He hit me with a roguish grin. "She happens to be one of my favorites."

She? "What does she look like?" Wait! Why was I asking such an inane question? What the hell did it matter?

Jaime twisted his mouth into a sly smile. "She's as hot as they come..."

Cringe.

"And gay." He smirked.

Bastard. He knew how to get to me.

He flicked a crumb of my croissant off my lips. "What are you planning to wear today?"

"Black leggings and an oversized heavy cashmere sweater." I wanted to be comfortable, but the sweats

I'd picked out earlier were way too casual for running around Paris.

"Sounds perfect, Matchy-matchy girl."

Polishing off his croissant, he stood up and strode back to my suitcase. Now what? One by one, he cherry-picked through my scanty lace bras and bikinis. A saucy smile played on his face as he examined each and every piece of the sexy lingerie. Mortification shot through me.

"What are doing?" My voice was shrill.

"What does it look like? I'm choosing your underwear."

"No way." This was going too far. I leaped up from my chair and stomped over to him. I snatched the matching leopard-print bra and thong out of his hands and flung them back into my suitcase.

"Come on, Gloria. Call it research. I'm getting a really good feel for the Gloria's Secret line...and for the woman behind it."

Wrinkling my nose, I looked him straight in the eyes. "And what does your research tell you about me?"

He nuzzled my sensitive neck. The sensation forced my head to arch and my eyelids to lower. I felt my robe sliding off my shoulders.

"Well, Mr. Zander, tell me." My body was heating up.

He slipped off my robe and purred in my ear. "That you're dripping with desire."

My breath hitched. He was right! I wanted him! Again!

"And I'm going to prove my theory."

In one swift move, he scooped me up in his arms

and tossed me onto the bed. Disrobing himself, he crashed upon me with all his weight, and in an instant, his cock was pounding inside me. Our breathing was haggard. My climax was building with the brutality and speed of an avalanche. I couldn't believe how fast he could make me come. With one final thrust, he spurted into me as I juddered around him.

"Holy fuck!" we moaned in unison.

Our sweat-slicked, heaving bodies stayed still in that position for several long minutes, allowing our breathing to calm down.

"Paris awaits us, angel," Jaime said brightly after smacking my lips with a kiss.

"Have you decided on what undies I should wear?" I asked coyly, threading my fingers through his tousled hair.

"Yeah...none."

My jaw slackened.

"I want to imagine you just the way you are all day long."

The feeling was mutual. My eyes never strayed from his gorgeous body, all golden cream and taut planes and angles, as he slipped on his faded jeans and tucked in his cock. His glorious, just-fucked cock.

We spent the day leisurely meandering through Paris, staying close to the Left Bank. Neither of us wanted to risk the chance of running into Victor, who never strayed from the Right Bank and would likely take his business meeting at The Intercontinental. The weather, like in New York, was surprisingly mild for this time of year. Global warming, I supposed. I couldn't complain, however, about the pleasant temperature and sunny sky.

We took in several of the famous Rive Gauche monuments—The Panthéon, The Sorbonne, Notre Dame to name a few. To be honest, I had never really gone sightseeing in Paris before. My trips, always rushed, were strictly for business—be it to catch a fashion show, explore new trends, or visit the Champs-Elysées store. Having this god-like tour guide beside me added to both the beauty and my enjoyment of the City of Light. As we strolled along the Seine, arm in arm, en route to The Louvre, I couldn't help noticing how many female heads he turned. I stole a glance at his face and could understand why. His profile with its strong dimpled chin, manly straight nose, and thick-lashed eyes was gorgeous. He still hadn't shaven—the thicker than usual layer of stubble making him even sexier. My heart fluttered. No man had ever had this effect on me. He had made me fall apart. And now, I was falling for him. In just one week, this man had captured me, both physically and emotionally. He was in my bloodstream, bringing me to new levels of sensuality and self-awareness I'd never known. Unable to get enough of him, I was worried about working with him professionally. The uncertainty of the future and the challenges ahead sent a shiver skittering down my spine. I had to admit—I was afraid of getting hurt, and the threat that both Victor and Vivien posed didn't help. I wished I could share everything with Madame Paulette. She'd know what to do. Her last words to me swirled around in my head. "It *eez* better to have loved..." I still wasn't sure what I felt. *Just enjoy the moment, Gloria*, I told myself, taking a deep breath as we approached the majestic Louvre.

Experiencing The Louvre with Jaime was something else and not just because every female tourist from eighteen to eighty had eyes for him as if he were some rare Greek statue. As we glided from one gallery of paintings to another, Jaime, who was truly more beautiful than any of the museum's god-like male sculptures, came alive like I'd never seen before. His blue eyes glistened, and his voice was animated as he explained the significance and details of each masterpiece.

"How do you know so much about art?" I asked him, in awe of his knowledge. It actually turned me on, but I wasn't going to share that with him.

"My father." His voice was coated with melancholy. "Though he never fulfilled his dream of coming to Paris, he took me to museums in Los Angeles and had tons of art books that he shared with me. He would play games with me—make me guess the name of a painter or race with him to find a particular painting. Or show me tricks."

"What kind of tricks?" I asked as we stood before the *Mona Lisa.*

"Look at the *Mona Lisa's* eyes. They'll follow yours."

I gazed at the painting and shifted my eyes to the right. Sure enough, the iconic beauty's eyes followed mine. "Wow! That's incredible!"

We continued to study the hypnotic painting.

"Who were your father's favorite painters?" I asked.

Jaime smiled wistfully. "He loved so many, but his favorite was Van Gogh."

"Why Van Gogh?"

"I think he connected to his tortured life...his inner demons."

The paintings I'd seen in both his office space and hotel suite flashed into my head. They had actually reminded me a lot of Van Gogh's work, with their vivid colors and turbulent strokes.

Seeking confirmation, I queried, "Those paintings in your office and at the hotel...did your father paint them?"

Jaime's smile widened. Pride washed over his face. "Yes. I'm glad you noticed them. When he died, I secretly gathered all his paintings and hid them in storage until I could display them. One day, when I have time, I'm going to exhibit them. I want my father to have the glory he deserved."

"They're pretty amazing."

"You're pretty amazing, Ms. Long."

Gripping my shoulders, he spun me around and crushed his beautifully etched lips onto mine with a bruising, passionate kiss. A moan escaped my throat as he deepened the kiss with his velvety tongue. Oh, God, he tasted divine! Our tongues danced, swirling together in figure eights. Tingles shot down my body, from my head to my toes. I swear if we weren't in a public place, I would have let this masterpiece of a man fuck me right here and now and let the *Mona*

Lisa watch with her magic eyes.

After a late lunch at a nearby café and another long, delicious tongue-driven kiss, Jaime and I went our separate ways. He to visit that client, who I still didn't trust, and I to visit the Gloria's Secret store on the busy Champs-Elysées.

I was happy to see that our first Paris store was bustling with customers. I took special satisfaction in knowing that even Parisian women were gobbling up our reasonably priced American-made lingerie when they had the most exquisite underwear in the world at their fingertips. I found Sandrine quickly. Dressed in head to toe black with the exception of a colorful silk scarf knotted around her neck, the slim, spiky-haired woman epitomized French chic. She was showing a young attractive sales girl how to re-stack bikinis and bras after they had been mussed up by customers. I found it so annoying that customers were often such slobs, with no sympathy for the low-paid, hard-working sales assistants who had to clean up after their damage.

Sandrine spotted me immediately and ran over to me with open arms. We exchanged a typically French double cheek embrace.

"*Ça va?*" she asked.

"*Ça va bien.*" I replied. "*Merci beaucoup* for helping me with Madame Paulette's burial."

"*Pas de problème.* I'm so sorry for your loss." Like many Europeans, Sandrine spoke perfect English though she liked to throw in a little French. I, in turn, could conduct a conversation with her in

French, thanks to Madame Paulette's tutelage.

Sandrine was one of my favorite and most respected store managers. She was bright, organized, and always one step ahead. She ran the store with both a smile and an iron fist. Recently, at the age of thirty-two, she had become engaged to a successful and handsome doctor.

"Do you have a little time? I'd love to take you out for a drink to thank you for helping me and to celebrate your engagement."

"For you, I always have *zee* time," she said brightly.

We ended up going to a lively café that was a few doors down from the store. Over champagne, we caught up on business and then moved on to personal stuff. She was getting married in April—it was going to be a big Jewish wedding at her family's country home in Provence.

"My *maman eez* driving me crazy!" she sighed. "Everything she loves, I detest. Can you imagine... she wants jars of butterflies on every table that *zee* guests will set free after we say our vows!"

I laughed lightly. "At least you have a mother who cares about you," I countered. A wistful expression fell over me. Sandrine was one of the few people, other than Kevin and Madame Paulette, who knew about my crack whore mother.

She twitched a guilty smile. "You're right. She means well." She sipped her champagne. "I hope you will come."

I let her know I wouldn't miss it for the world. Her smile brightened.

"What about you, Gloria? *Eez* there anyone new

in your life?"

Blushing, I shook my head and said, "Not really."

"Gloria, I don't believe you. Your face gives *eet* away. Spill *zee* beans as you Americans say."

Draining my champagne, I broke down and told her all about Jaime—including the complications with Victor and Vivien, who she openly despised.

"Mon dieu! This *eez* heavy. But I would have given my tongue to *zee* cat to see Vivien's expression when she saw you and Jaime kissing at *zee* restaurant. *La putain!"*

I couldn't stop laughing. She'd just called Vivien a whore! Like Kevin, Sandrine could be so brutally honest. And a bit wicked. That's why I adored her.

"So what does Monsieur Zahn-deur look like?"

The way she breathily said his name with her French accent sent me over the moon. I described Jaime to her, from head to foot, as if we were a painting in The Louvre. The words came so easy. In my mind, he was a work of art.

"He sounds like a hottie!"

I giggled. Usually the word "hottie" made me cringe, but the way she said it—HAH-tee—was charming. My cheeks heated.

My delightful French friend and colleague took a sip of her champagne. "Gloria, are you in love with him?"

"I've only known him for a week."

"You didn't answer my question."

A loud sigh escaped my lungs.

"Ah, Gloria, you are! You are! *Mazel tov!"*

I remembered Madame Paulette once telling me that sometimes *l'amour* slinks up to you like a cat; other times it attacks you like a lion. Jaime Zander was a sexy beast who had all but consumed me. I could no longer deny my feelings. Yes, I was hopelessly, helplessly head over heels in love with him.

My heart began to roar at the very thought of him touching me. Longing and lust surged through my body. I grasped my friend's French manicured hand and murmured, "Sandrine, what should I do?"

"It *eez* simple. Don't let him go."

I smiled back. It never ceased to amaze me how wise French women were.

"But don't tell him you love him until he tells *eet* to you." More words of wisdom.

The check came. As we hugged good-bye, my sage friend whispered into my ear, "I'll see the future Monsieur and Madame Zahn-deur at my wedding."

When I got back to our hotel room, three dozen long-stemmed red roses, arranged in three tall crystal vases, awaited me. My heart melted. Mr. Zander was true to his word and a romantic.

I dipped my nose into one of the bouquets and inhaled deeply. The scent was divine. Intoxicating just like him.

"Hey."

At the sound of his voice, I straightened up and caught sight of him stepping out of the bathroom. He was wearing nothing but a white towel wrapped around his hips. My eyes zeroed in on the deep "V" that emanated from it and then traveled up over his washboard abs and toned pecs. My gaze met his, and my breathing hitched.

"They're beautiful!"

"My biceps?"

Conceited fuck! I scrunched my nose.

"No, the roses."

"Thanks." He cocked a bashful smile as though the flowers were an embarrassing afterthought. Our eyes stayed locked on one another. Silence. My sex was throbbing, my heart pounding. I wanted to be lost in him. Neither of us moved. The seconds felt like hours.

"Get over here, you," he said at last, and in a heartbeat, I was in his arms. We were at each other as if an apocalypse was dawning. Kissing, groping, stroking, licking. He lifted my sweater up over my head, unable to get it off fast enough. Panting, I kicked off my ballet flats and said good-bye to my leggings. The towel fell off his torso, and we were fused together, flesh to flesh. With his mouth locked on mine, he walked me backward until I was sandwiched between him and a wall.

"Wrap your legs around me, angel," he said, lifting me off my feet.

Our eyes level, I did as he asked, looping my long legs around his waist and my arms around his neck. He gripped my ass to support me. Between my thighs, I felt his hot cock line up with my opening. "Gloria, you don't know how badly I've wanted to have you like this."

"Shut up and fuck me." I couldn't believe my own words. I was begging for him.

"I'm going to give it to you hard."

Oh, yes!

"Promise me you'll scream my name like it's the only word you know."

"Girl Scout's honor!" I gasped even though I'd never been one.

Satisfied, he pounded into me with a powerful thrust, pushing me into the wall with the weight of his body. We both cried out with carnal pleasure. As he got into a rhythm, he latched his hungry lips back onto mine and I moved my hands to his face, possessively cupping his stubbled jaw. Our kiss deepened, our tongues locking together in a fierce sensuous dance. We moaned and groaned into each other's mouths.

Our hips collided like bumper cars with each forceful strike. As he picked up momentum, I squeezed my thighs tighter around him to hang on. My breasts skimmed his chest, and my clit pressed tight against his pubic bone, making the sensation of every deep thrust so much more intense. In no time, I was a sweaty, whimpering bundle of bliss on the verge of a major orgasm.

"Angel, I can't fucking get enough of you," he panted against my mouth.

And I couldn't get enough of him. The words, "I love you," were on the tip of my tongue, but I bit down on it to hold them in. Sandrine was right. He had to say them first. I drank in his sexy, heated face, longing for those three little words to form on his lips.

"Is this hard enough for you?" he asked instead, powering into me repeatedly.

"Yes!" I cried. I was losing every ounce of control, a mere breath away from detonating.

"Good. I'm going to give you what you want." He rewarded with me with a pinch of my clit, and that's all it took. Everything inside me clenched, and I exploded, shuddering against the wall and screaming his name for the first time over and over.

"Oh, Gloria," he roared as his own forceful climax met mine. I could feel him jerk three times, his hot release pouring down my already drenched thighs. He rested his glistening forehead on mine, our shallow breaths mingling.

"Fuck, Gloria. That was even better than I'd imagined," he said hoarsely.

Confession: Wall banging was something I'd fantasized about ever since he'd mentioned it in his conference room. It'd exceeded my expectations too. It was like a thrill ride—the kind you thought you'd fall off if you didn't hold on tight and left you breathless, wanting to do it all over again.

His breathing almost back to normal, he gathered my limp, glistening body into his arms and licked his upper lip. "I'm not done with you, Ms. Long."

This man was insatiable. Though spent, I wasn't done with him either. I wanted more. As he carried me away, a wildfire burnt inside me, consuming every part of me. Sandrine was right. Even if he hadn't said the three magic words, I couldn't let him go.

We fucked our brains out again in the shower and then we hopped into his bed, minty clean, naked, and wasted. He spooned me into his body, wrapping one sculpted arm around my chest. The deft fingers of his other hand glided along my folds.

"You're always wet for me, Gloria."

"You're not going to fuck me again?" I asked, trying to imagine what it would feel like in this cuddly position. It felt delicious to be blanketed by his warm body, and I was quite frankly unsure if could handle another mind-blowing assault.

He nuzzled the nape of my neck. "No, angel, not even if you begged for it. We need to rest up for dinner and the surprise I have in store."

"What kind of surprise?" The word made me buzz with lust and curiosity.

"Come on, it wouldn't be a surprise if I told you. Now, close your eyes."

Obeying him, I was shrouded in his scent, his breath, his touch. I reflected on this shift in power. Being dominated by a man was something new for me—uncharted territory. As I drifted off, I had to admit I was more than enjoying it. I loved it. And I loved him. Only one question weighed on my heart: Did he love me?

The restaurant Jaime took me to was an intimate neighborhood bistro, walking distance from the hotel. With its candlelit, red-checkered tablecloth tables and funky outsider art on the walls, it was definitely not the kind of restaurant where you'd find Victor Holden. Chances were he was holding court with his business associate and some hired high-priced female escorts at some posh club on the Right Bank.

We sat side by side like true Parisians along

a red leather banquet. His thigh brushed against mine and our shoulders touched. When he turned to speak or look at me, his warm breath grazed my flesh. He smelled delicious and looked sinfully sexy. He was clad in all black—elegantly tailored, belted wool slacks and a form-fitting cashmere sweater that clung to his prominent biceps and showed off broad, chiseled chest. Mr. Fucking Continental! I was wearing my blue chiffon dress, the one I'd worn when we went to dinner in New York with matching blue lace lingerie. Jaime had insisted I wear it along with my hair down; the least I could do was oblige. It was a small concession but nonetheless piqued my curiosity.

"Why this outfit?" I asked after a sip of the expensive Côtes du Rhône white wine he'd ordered.

"Because, Ms. Long, it makes you very surprise-worthy."

A shiver zigzagged down my spine. He still hadn't given me a clue into the surprise he had planned. Though I was sure it had to with lifting up the skirt of my dress and doing some very naughty things. My core tingled at the thought of the possibilities.

While the meal in front of me, a delicate poisson au beurre, looked delectable, I had a hard time eating it when I knew this gorgeous man was totally eye-fucking me. His denim blue eyes burnt into mine. Wetness rushed to my core, and my cheeks flushed in embarrassment.

He smirked at me, knowing damn well he was affecting me. I kept waiting for him to make a move. The surprise. My gaze drank in his searing eyes and that sexy, slightly parted mouth that was longing for a taste of me. My body was crackling all over with anticipation. Seated so intimately close to each other, a kiss was just inches away. And that was just for starters.

I finally managed a bite of my fish. It was delicious. Jaime watched as I savored the flavorful, buttery fillet.

"So how did you learn to fuck, Gloria?" he asked before I could swallow.

I almost gagged. I was certainly not prepared for that conversation game changer.

Genetics. My mother was a crack whore.

"I've been around," I managed after regaining my composure and feeling assured I wouldn't regurgitate my food. We turned at once to face each other.

He cocked a brow. "What does that mean?"

"I fucked a lot of guys when I moved to LA."

"Anyone serious?"

"No just a bunch of fucks." Heartless fucks—none of which had ever given me an orgasm. Even a mild one. It was a just stupid phase I went through to keep my mind off the heinous crime I'd committed back East. My secret. Once Gloria's Secret took off, I had little time for any kind of sexual relationship.

"What about that PR guy of yours?"

"You mean, Kevin?"

"Yeah. He's very good-looking, and seems like he's really into you."

"He happens to be my best friend. He also happens to be gay." *And he's fucking your assistant Ray.*

A wry smile flickered on his face. "Good. That's

what I thought. I don't want to share you with anyone." He sipped his wine. "And what about that boyfriend you were visiting in New York?"

My eyes widened. I thought he'd seen right through my pathetic white lie, but maybe he'd given it second thought. *Score one for me.*

I took a long slug of wine to keep him in suspense.

He tugged at my hair. His face tensed. "Well..."

Okay, enough torture. "You don't have to worry about him."

"Good. You know, I'm very possessive. I'll knock his teeth out and make it so he'll never be able to put his mouth to yours ever."

"You won't have to," I reassured him, both intimidated and turned on by his violent, jealous streak. After another morsel of fish, I asked, "And what about you, Mr. Zander? It's only fair that I get some more insight into your social life."

He grinned. "You mean, sex life." A statement, not a question.

"Semantics." I wrinkled my nose at him, knowing that turned him on.

"Let's put it this way. I've probably fucked every model in your Gloria's Secret catalogue."

I almost choked again. Why should I be surprised?

"But just like you, they were only mindless fucks."

That wasn't good enough. "That could pose another major conflict of interest." Jealousy scorched through me, thinking that whoever we cast in the new advertising campaign might be someone he'd fucked. Or wanted to fuck. I shuddered at the thought of being just another conquest...the newest member on his find-feel-fuck-and-forget list.

With a roguish glint in his eyes, Mr. God's Gift to Models twisted a lock of my loose hair around his index finger. "Don't worry, Gloria. I plan to use fresh talent. In fact, I'm still convinced that *you* should be the star."

What?

His eyes traveled from my face to my cleavage and stayed there. "My creative instincts tell me it just feels right."

I raised my brows. "I don't get it."

"Think about it, angel. A beautiful, sexy CEO selling what she believes in. It would be breakthrough. And trust me, a camera couldn't take a bad shot of you. We'll just have to airbrush that scar of yours that you won't tell me about."

That did it. Before I could ingest another bite of the fish, I choked. Turning red, I immediately reached for my sparkling water and gulped it down.

"Are you okay?" asked a concerned Jaime.

"I don't think so," I finally managed, trying to wash down the painful memory.

"Do you want me to take you back to the hotel?"

"No. I'm fine. I meant about me modeling for the ad campaign."

Jaime looked relieved. "Trust me, you'll change your mind." He leaned into me and planted a chaste kiss on my lips, his first physical advance thus far. I inwardly trembled, still reeling from his obsession with my scar and his sexploits. I also wondered if this kiss would lead to my surprise. Any form of sex in this small intimate restaurant made my nerves sizzle.

To my relief, his advances stopped with the kiss. He continued to talk business, focusing on the timeline and logistics of the shoot. I half-listened, too wrapped up with my newfound insecurities. Feelings never entered the conversation. I was glad when the check came and reached for it.

"Remember, I still owe you a dinner."

He grabbed the check out of my hand. "No, Gloria. Let me pay. I'll charge it back to your account as I would call this strictly a business dinner."

"Fine." I flung the word at him as he dug into a pocket for his credit card and slapped it onto the table.

Our waiter returned with the paid bill. Jaime had obviously tipped him well because he had brought us our outerwear that we'd left with the coat-check. Rising, Jaime shrugged on his leather bomber jacket; it was the one he wore when I first met him. One look at him in it made him once again totally irresistible. He adjusted my shawl over my shoulders, reverently lifting up my blanket of hair as he did. I put my doubts aside. By his actions— oh, those roses!—and the amount of time he spent with me, I had to be believe I was different from the others. He even said I was.

He kissed a sensitive spot on the side of my neck, bringing me into the moment. "So, Ms. Long, are you ready for your surprise?"

Ten minutes later, I was huddled next to him in his limo, blindfolded with a dense piece of black lace, heading to an unknown destination.

"Where are we going?" I asked nervously, brushing against his soft leather jacket as the limo made a sharp turn.

"That, my angel, *is* the surprise."

Chapter 14

A SHORT FIFTEEN MINUTES LATER, I found myself traipsing across what my other senses told me was a pebbly path in my six-inch stilettos. Except for the crunching sounds of our footsteps and sirens in the distance, the balmy Paris air was silent. Damn it! I wished I could see where he was taking me.

"Why did you have to blindfold me?" I asked, clutching his arm for balance.

"Gloria, shame on you. You should know the answer to that already. To learn to trust me."

My eyes rolled under the blindfold. Distracted, one of my sharp heels caught in the gravel. I stumbled but he caught me. "Are you taking me to some private underground sex club?" I asked nervously.

He laughed heartily. "Close but no cigar. It's definitely private, but underground is the last word I'd use to describe it."

What the fuck? Beneath my lace blindfold, my nose scrunched. "Are we there yet?" I asked, silently berating myself for sounding like a whiny six-year-old on a road trip.

"Patience has its virtues, Ms. Long," he replied, picking up our pace to my chagrin.

Several steps later, I could hear music. A familiar

song, one of Madame Paulette's favorites. "Toi et Moi" sung by Charles Aznavour.

"*Bonsoir,* Monsieur Zander. I have been looking forward to seeing you again."

A Frenchman's deep, jovial voice sounded in my ears. We must be at our destination, I thought.

"*Bonsoir*, Claude. Are we set to go?"

"*Oui, monsieur*. Up, up, and away. You and *zee* beautiful *mademoiselle* can board *tout de suite.*"

My stomach bunched up with nerves. Was he taking me on a private plane? Or on a helicopter? Or a hot air balloon? Flying in an airplane was bad enough, but a chopper? That flimsy whirling flying machine? Even worse...a hot air balloon that could hit a power line and explode in mid air. I bit down on my lip. Oh, God. Is that what he had in store?

"I'm afraid of flying!" I gasped. My hand grew cold and clammy in his.

Jaime yanked me unceremoniously away, I assumed, in the direction of the aircraft; I resisted, clumsily tripping a couple of times in my heels along the way.

"Relax, Gloria. You're going to be flying all right but not the kind you have in mind." He led the way. "Watch your head and your step."

Too late. Instead of ducking, I banged my head hard as I climbed over some mysterious threshold. I let out a loud "OW."

"Are you okay?" asked Jaime. There was humor in his voice, like he was holding back laughter. *Insensitive jerk!*

"Yes," I grumbled, rubbing the already forming bump with my free hand. I hesitantly took a few more steps.

"Sit," he commanded, pressing down on my shoulders.

I slowly lowered my butt to a hard, lightly cushioned surface and then explored my surroundings with both hands like a blind person, tapping, touching, and absorbing everything around me. I was sitting on some kind of bench, surrounded by glass. Was I in some kind of elevator? Enough with the blindfold! But when I raised my hands to my head, Jaime grasped them midway and stopped me. He was definitely sitting across from me.

"Uh, uh, uh," he chided playfully. "Don't make me tie you up. I've got another lace binding right here in my pocket. It'll only take me seconds to wrap it around those lovely hands of yours."

"Sorry," I said meekly. *Asshole!*

"Promise you won't undo the blindfold?" He squeezed my hands so tight I yelped.

"Promise." Why did I continue to submit to his little sadistic power games? Damn it. Why? The answer was simple: I was still crazy in love with him.

"Enjoy your ride," said Claude.

I heard two gliding doors slide closed. *Clink!*

"Where are we going?" I asked anxiously.

"You'll see soon enough." Despite being blindfolded, I could see the smirk on his smug face.

Suddenly, we jerked. I jolted. And then swoop! My stomach fluttered. We were going up! Up and around! Holy fuck! The butterflies inside me multiplied as we rose higher and higher. The spinning sensation was familiar. I had an idea of where I was. My heart began to race, and sweat seeped out of my pores. I was having a panic attack.

Sixty long seconds later, the spinning came to a halt. Jaime yanked off my blindfold.

"Open your eyes, Gloria," he commanded, his voice deep and sultry.

I flicked my eyes open and gasped. I was suspended high in the air, seated opposite a very smug Jaime Zander. My heart pitter-pattered. Oh my God! I was trapped in a cabin with this gorgeous god on Paris's famed Ferris wheel, the Grande Roue. At a standstill at the very apex—as high as the wheel could go.

I was at a loss for words. A combination of terror, outrage, and pure awe consumed me. Surrounded by glass on all sides, I took in the twinkling lights of Paris—The City of Light—below. The view took my breath away.

I finally found my voice. "How did you manage this?"

Jaime's lush mouth curled into a proud, cocky smile. "My client. She's the head of the French Tourism Bureau. The advertising campaign I created for her last year resulted in a fifty percent spike in tourism. She was beholden to me and told me she owed me. Anything I wanted...and *voilà*, Mademoiselle Long, here we are."

The cabin suddenly rocked. I let out a frightened gasp. Jaime clasped my hands in his. "Relax, Gloria. This is going to be fun. The thrill ride of your life."

"I don't do well with Ferris wheels," I gulped. Like airplanes and high-speed elevators, they were one of those things that made me feel out of control.

When I was a teenager living close to Brooklyn's Coney Island, I had once ridden the amusement park's famed Ferris wheel, and it had gotten stuck, leaving me helplessly trapped in the swinging open-air carriage on the top. The memory of that dreadful experience made me tremble.

Jaime squeezed my hands. "Take a deep breath, angel. You're going to do just fine with me. What do you think of the view?"

Inhaling, I pressed my face against a glass pane. "It's spectacular," I managed, my eyes lingering on the lit up Eiffel Tower.

"No, Gloria. I meant this view."

My gaze jumped back to his beautiful face and followed his eyes as they led me to his crotch.

Holy fuck! Another tower of steel sprung into view. Jaime's monumental cock!

"Well...?"

"It's spectacular!" I repeated as tingles shot down to my flooding core. My inner muscles began to clench. *Holy, holy fuck!*

"Good. I want you to enjoy it." A broad, saucy grin spread across his face. He gestured with his long forefinger. "Get over here, you."

My legs jelly, I hesitantly stood up and staggered over to him, bending so as not to bang my head again. Thank goodness, the cabin had stopped rocking.

My heartbeat quickened. I knew what was next. "Do you want me to suck you?"

Sure of his response, I lowered myself to my knees. But before they could hit the floor, he yanked me upright by my hair.

"Not this time, angel."

I stared at him blankly.

"Sit on me!" A command.

In a breath, he lifted up my sheer dress and— *Slash!*—tore off my lacy blue bikinis. All that remained was the matching lace garter and attached sheer silk stockings. I was very exposed. A finger slid across my wet folds, sending sparks of pleasure to my core. He sucked on it and then ran it across the wide rim of his erection.

"Perfect!" Planting his manly hands firmly on my waist, he positioned me exactly where he wanted me to be, straddling his rock-hard thighs and...

Impaled on his giant cock! I moaned as his hot girth, that magnificent tower, speared into me, filling me to the hilt. Oh. My. God.

His denim blue eyes, now fiery and fierce, bore into mine. His hot breath heated my already flaming face.

"Aren't you going to tie me up?" I immediately regretted my words. I wasn't thinking straight.

"Hey, angel, no need; there's no place to go... except down on me." He lifted me up a few inches by my hips and dragged his hard throbbing shaft down my wet tunnel. His cock immediately bucked back up me, so deep I yelped.

"And besides, you'll need your hands. Hold on to my shoulders."

I slapped my palms onto them, curling my fingers around the bone-hard edges. A gasp escaped my throat as he lifted me again.

"Now, ride me, angel! Hard!"

I crashed down on his slick thickness, then

immediately lifted my hips and descended hard on him again. We instantly got into a rhythm. Up and down. Up and down. I loved every thrust. Now, this was a thrill ride! I kept pace with him as he bucked harder and faster. My breasts brushed up and down his leather jacket, the friction sending heat waves to my core. Beneath the lace of my bra, I could feel my nipples swelling and hardening. His eyes grew hooded, his breathing ragged. I was riding him to heaven. I chewed my lip to hold back whimpers.

He bit my upper lip, and my mouth parted from the delicious pain.

"It's okay to scream," he said, his voice low and sultry. "No one's going to hear you up here except me."

Suddenly, the wheel started spinning again. He gripped my hips tighter, for sure bruising my skin, as I clung to his shoulders, still riding him. We were descending to earth but I was ascending skyward. My head was spinning out of control and so was my core. I couldn't help screaming. The whirling dervish of sensations that swirled inside me was bringing me to the edge. Let me rephrase...this was one *extreme* thrill ride.

"I need to come!" I pleaded, hot tears now trickling down my cheeks. Even my aching thighs were crying out for relief.

"Not yet." He could barely manage the two words, his breathing so ragged.

Ruthlessly, relentlessly, he continued pounding into me as I posted and met his every thrust. This man had no mercy. His face contorted, and moans filled the cabin. The intense pressure inside me was building. Building so fast I thought I'd implode. I squeezed my eyes shut.

"Gloria, open your eyes. Now!"

I forced them open.

"Don't take them off the Eiffel Tower."

A heartbeat away from coming, I focused my gaze on the Paris landmark. My mouth dropped open, forming a big O, as the monumental tower burst into a shower of scintillating white light. At that very moment, my own shower of titillating sparks burst inside me, zapping every inch of my being.

"Oh my God, oh my God, oh my God," I screamed over and over as the sparks kept flying.

"Gloria, now watch me light up." He turned my head away from the window to face him.

My eyes met his for a brief second. His face distorted with tortuous rapture as he rammed into me one more time.

"Oh my God," I shrieked again as his electrifying explosion met mine fast and furious with a roar of my name. I collapsed onto his chest, dazed and totally awed that this sex god had so skillfully managed to orchestrate our orgasms with the Eiffel Tower's own orgasmic spectacle of lights.

"Oh, angel," he groaned, his voice hoarse, and his still flickering dick going nowhere. "That was so fucking amazing."

I responded with the only three words I seemed to know. "Oh. My. God."

He pulled me off his chest with a fistful of my hair and held me in his gaze. "My turn to enjoy the view. You're so beautiful after a good fuck." His pouted lips latched onto mine, sucking and gnawing until my mouth parted and met his tongue, stroke for stroke. My hands left his shoulders and cupped his beautiful face. The touch of the stubble along his jawline brought feeling back to my nearly numb, stiff fingers. Though my eyes were closed, I could still see and feel the sparks inside me. His cock, still buzzing, didn't budge. We were totally lost in one another.

A scraping thud brought us back to reality. The spinning wheel came to a halt. We were at last back on the ground although my mind and body were still spinning wildly somewhere in space. Jaime slowly withdrew his tongue, and then his slick, swollen cock, tucking it inside his slacks. After zipping his fly, he helped straighten my dress so that it covered my legs in a lady-like way. My shredded bikinis by my ankles were now part of French history.

I was still in a daze, sitting on his lap with my arms clasped around his neck, when the cabin doors automatically slid open. My heart jumped. Claude!

"One more spin?" he asked. The mischievous twinkle in his dark eyes clued me that he knew what had gone down up there. I flushed with embarrassment, acutely aware of the wetness between my legs.

Jaime winked at the robust, mustached man. "Take it away, Claude."

My heart leapt into my throat. Holy shit! He was going to fuck my brains out again and send me orbiting back into space? I tensed up.

"Are you going to—?"

He cut me off with a fierce kiss that made me melt.

Pulling away, he shot me a wry smile and twirled a clump of my hair. He hadn't done that for a while.

"Gloria, I overestimate you and you underestimate me. Do you really think a creative guy like me would do the same thing twice?"

I screwed up my face. "Well, to be honest—"

He cut me off again. "To be honest, I just want to hold you this time around." He coaxed me to sink my head against his warm, tight chest. I sighed as I melted into him. The sweet musky smell of his leather jacket wafted up my nose. I closed my eyes to the song of our heartbeats thrumming together. *Heaven!*

When we got to the top, the cabin began to rock again. Blissfully, I just let myself rock with him, swathed by the warmth of his body. The rise and fall of his chest and the sound of his soft breathing lulled me into a trance-like state. I felt so safe when I should have felt so scared. I'd lost track of time when he nuzzled my neck, bringing awareness back into me.

"Gloria," he whispered into my ear. "I have another surprise for you."

Another surprise? What now? He never ceased to amaze me. Slowly, I lifted my head from his chest and met his gaze. His eyes were twinkling like the lights below us. He circled my lips with his index finger and then dug his hand into a pocket of his jacket. He whipped out a small red velvet box and held it in his palm. "Open it, Gloria," he ordered. "It'll turn you on."

A mixture of curiosity and anticipation coursed through me as I took the box from him. What could be inside? A butt plug? A nipple clamp? A clit ring? I was familiar with ali of these little sex toys from our research for our new product line but knew nothing about them personally. With jittery fingers, I flicked it open. I gaped in shock and my heart skipped a beat. Glaring in my eyes was a magnificent platinum ring with two entwined, heart-shaped diamonds. They sparkled like the stars surrounding us. I couldn't get my mouth to close.

"Do you know what this is?" asked Jaime, his eyes burning into mine.

My heart was slamming so hard against my chest I thought it would leap out. "Are you asking me to marry you?"

TO BE CONTINUED

Gloria and Jaime's story concludes in
the steamy and suspenseful sequel...

Gloria's Revenge
Available Now

Acknowledgments

A big shout-out to Team Gloria...

My beta readers in alphabetical order...Michele Coddington, Adriane Leigh, Cindy Meyer, and Jen Oreto. You were invaluable!

My you-know-who-you-are dear Facebook and Twitter fans whose kind words got me through the long, difficult edit.

My cover artist and formatter, Glendon Haddix of Streetlight Graphics.

My proofreader, Kathie Middlemiss of Kat's Eye Editing.

My family. I know you all roll your eyes at me for all the time I spend at my computer, but it brings food to our table. And gives me validity.

I also want to express my gratitude to all my readers. Without you, I don't exist. I hope you enjoyed *Gloria's Secret* and will take the time to leave a review.

Thank you all from the bottom of my heart.

MWAH!~Nelle

About The Author

Nelle L'Amour is a bestselling *New York Times* and *USA. Today* author who lives in Los Angeles with her Prince Charming-ish husband, twin teenage princesses, and a bevy of royal pain-in-the-butt pets. A former executive in the entertainment and toy industries with a prestigious Humanitas Award to her credit, she gave up playing with Barbies a long time ago, but still enjoys playing with toys... with her husband. While she writes in her PJ's, she loves to get dressed up and pretend she's Hollywood royalty. She aspires to write juicy stories with characters that will make you both laugh and cry and stay in your heart forever.

She is also a bestselling author of the critically acclaimed erotic love story, *Undying Love*, and the erotic romance series, *Seduced by the Park Avenue Billionaire*. Writing under another pen name, she is the author of the highly rated fantasy/romance *Dewitched: The Untold Story of the Evil* Queen and its sequel, *Unhitched*.

Nelle loves to hear from her readers. Connect to her at:

nellelamour@gmail.com
www.facebook.com/NelleLamourAuthor
www.twitter.com/nellelamour

Bonus

I hope you will check out my bestselling erotic love story that so many readers and bloggers have called beautiful—*Undying Love.*

Here is a snippet:

Allee didn't touch her wine. Instead, she scrutinized my face, zeroing in on the Band-Aid on my forehead. "So, Golden Boy, what the hell happened to your face?"

Although I really was tired of talking about it, I was glad she had started some form of conversation.

"Shaving mishap." Embarrassment mixed with shakiness as I flashed back to my violent breakup with Charlotte.

"Bullshit. I don't know any guys who shave their forehead." She paused as she studied my face further. "It was her. That blond psycho-bitch."

I grimaced. "Yeah."

"Your girlfriend? She looks like your type."

"Ex-girlfriend." It actually felt good to say that. Liberating.

She nodded pensively and took a sip of her wine. It was hard to tell what she was thinking. Finally, she said, "I hope she looks worse."

I couldn't help smiling. Her wicked sense of humor made her even sexier.

"So, Madewell, tell me something I don't know about your life."

She hardly knew a thing about my life. I told her how I was born into privilege, or at least that's how others perceived it. Actually, it was more a life of neglect. "My mother was never there for me, and I literally had to make appointments with my father to see him."

"That's whacked." She chuckled. Her laugh was deep and sexy, and it made me smile again. I continued.

"My sister and I were raised by our nanny, Maria. I think if she hadn't been there for us, we would have run away or turned to drugs. She was loving and kept us grounded. When I turned thirteen, my parents sent me off to boarding school—Andover."

She snorted. "Bet they couldn't wait to get rid of you."

"Yeah. Seriously, if there was a boarding school for preschoolers, I would have been there."

She laughed again. I liked the fact that she enjoyed my sense of humor. Charlotte never had, finding my off-color comments totally unnecessary.

"So then what, Golden Boy?"

"No choice. Off to my father's alma mater, Harvard. He wanted me to major in finance. I wanted to major in English. After a long battle, we finally compromised. He let me major in English as an undergraduate as long as I went to Harvard Business School for grad school. His goal has always been to groom me to take over Madewell Media when he retires."

"And is that what you want to do?" asked Allee,

leaning in closer to me.

"No. I want to be a novelist. But that's never going to happen. Okay, your turn."

Allee's life story was so different from mine yet, in some ways, so similar. At the age of three, she lost her parents, both artists, in a tragic auto accident. From that point on, she went in and out of the foster care system, landing with one unloving family after another. We were both orphans of sorts. What kept her going was education and books. She dreamed and worked hard, earning the grades to get her a partial scholarship and student loan to Parsons, a college known for its fine arts program. On a field trip to the Met in high school, she had fallen in love with art and vowed one day that she would work in a museum.

"Who are your favorite painters?" I asked, intrigued by her passion.

"I know it's mundane, but I love the French Impressionists. The Madewell Gallery is awesome, but it can't compare to the Met's Impressionist collection. I could hang out with those paintings all day." Her face grew dreamy, and there was yet another level of beauty to her. I think she had no clue how beautiful she was, even in that drab Met uniform.

"Why haven't you been to Paris?"

Her face turned somber. "I was almost going to go there my junior year in college."

"Why didn't you?" I immediately regretted my question because it probably had something to do with not being able to afford it.

She hesitated, running her forefinger around

the rim of the wine glass. "I had to deal with some personal shit."

My eyes widened. "Like what?"

She drained her wine. "Oh, just some crap I don't want to think about." Her eyes darted to the right. "Hey, look, here come the chicken potpies."

She was obviously glad to change the subject. And I wasn't about to pursue an obviously sensitive issue this early on in the game. We both dug into the steaming dishes. I admired the gusto with which she devoured her crusty pie. So unlike Charlotte, who picked at her food (usually meager salads) like a bird. She even wiped the bottom clean with a chunk of bread.

"Dessert?" I asked.

"Sure...if we split it."

I ordered one of those delicious hot fudge sundaes that I so fondly remembered from my childhood. When the waiter set it down on our table, my eyes widened. It looked to be everything I remembered it to be. A mouthwatering, overflowing glass of vanilla ice cream, gooey fudge, and whipped cream.

"Do you want the cherry?" I asked Allee, remembering how my sister and I used to fight over it.

"Nope." She lifted the bright red candied fruit off the heap of whipped cream by its stem and then twirled it around. "Open your mouth," she ordered.

Taken aback, I did as she asked. She sensuously brushed the cherry around my lips and then dropped it into my mouth. "Swallow."

Another command. I swallowed it whole. Jesus! The cherry thing was having a strange effect on me.

I was getting a serious hard on! Plus, it gave me X-ray vision. I could see Allee's tits right through her blazer and blouse. They were full and firm, dotted with rosebuds the diameter of the cherry I'd just consumed. I had the insatiable urge to tear off her uniform, lather the whipped cream all over her breasts and then lick it off.

"What are you waiting for, Madewell?" she said. Holy fuck! Was she a mind reader?

Her lips curled up into a saucy, dimpled smile that made me want her more. "The ice cream's gonna melt."

I was what was melting. Distracted by my arousal, I dug one of the long sundae spoons deep into the mountain of whipped cream and scooped up a heaping of vanilla ice cream that was dripping with rich chocolate fudge.

"Taste," I said. My turn to be in charge.

She parted her lush lips, and I slipped the spoon into her mouth. She clamped her lips over the spoon and moaned. It was such a deep, sensual sound that I felt my erection press against my jeans.

After savoring the creamy ice cream a little longer, she spread her lips. I slowly glided out the spoon.

"Mmm. That was so good."

"Let me give you another taste." I was getting off on feeding her.

"No, Madewell. Let me feed you." She reached for the other spoon and filled my mouth with a heaping portion of the hot fudge sundae. It was every bit as good as I remembered it. My eyes met Allee's. There was only one thing my mouth watered for more —

her velvety tongue.

We continued this sensuous back and forth feeding until we were scraping the bottom of the sundae glass. I don't think I had ever shared a dessert with Charlotte as long as I'd known her.

Before the check came, I asked Allee if she wanted anything else.

"Yes." She smiled wickedly.

A coffee?

"I want to suck you, Madewell."

The temperature in the restaurant suddenly rose ten degrees, and my already hard cock boinged under my jeans.

My eyes stayed wide as she gracefully slid under the table. I squirmed as she unzipped my fly. My dick shot out. She wrapped her moist, sweet lips around the crown and rolled her tongue, chilled from the ice cream, around it. Holy shit! She knew how to give good head!

Slowly, her mouth descended on the hard, thick shaft and I could feel my cock growing bigger, filling the hollows of her cheeks. I was shocked by how much of me she could take in. When she reached the base, she slid her mouth back up and then right back down, her velvety tongue trailing along the back of the shaft. I arched my back and dug my fingers into the leather banquet. The elderly woman in the booth next to ours looked away from her book and eyed me strangely. God knows what she was thinking. As Allee went down on me again, I chewed my lip to stifle a groan. She picked up her pace, exerting gentle pressure with her teeth. My cock was throbbing. A tingling feeling spread from my head to my toes, and my face felt flush. The pressure was quickly becoming unbearable. I was building to a climax. On her next visit to my crown, her tongue flicked the tip. I helplessly could not hold off. My cock spasmed, and I pumped into her mouth with a hiss of relief. She lapped up my release with her tongue as if were creamy, flavorful ice cream. Jesus. I had just gone to heaven. Charlotte had never done this to me. Never. She actually found oral sex repulsive. With a final titillating lick of my dick, Allee zipped up my fly and magically reappeared, her glasses perched atop her head. The little old lady across the way gaped, like she was about to have a coronary. Allee licked her upper lip and shot her a wicked smile. I stifled my laughter.

Man, this girl was too much. The check came before I could say a word. "Let me take care of dinner." That was the least thing I could do for the mind-blowing blow job she'd given me. She reached for it before I could and, from her purse, pulled out two crisp twenty-dollar bills. "My treat," she said brightly.

18655536R00146

Printed in Great Britain
by Amazon